Atlas of
The Arab-Israeli Wars,
The Chinese Civil War,
and The Korean War

Thomas E. Griess
Series Editor

AVERY PUBLISHING GROUP INC.
Wayne, New Jersey

ISBN 0-89529-320-X

Contents

Table of Symbols

BASIC SYMBOLS

Battalion . . . .   **I I**

Regiment . . . .   **I I I**

Brigade . . . .   **X**

Division, air division . . . .   **X X**

Corps . . . .   **X X X**

Army, air force, fleet . . . .   **X X X X**

Army group . . . .   **X X X X X**

Airborne . . . .   ⌂

Air Force unit . . . .   ∞

Armor . . . .   ▭

Artillery . . . .   ▫

Cavalry . . . .   ▱

Infantry . . . .   ⊠

Mechanized . . . .   ⊠

Naval troops, ground employment . . . .   ⚓

Special naval landing force . . . . . .   SNLF

OTHER SYMBOLS

	Actual location	Prior location
Troops on the march		
Troops in position		
	Occupied	Unoccupied
Troops in bivouac or reserve		
Field works		
Strong prepared positions		
Airfield		
Covering force, armor or foot		

Troops in position under attack . . . .

Route of march or flight . . . .

Boundary between units . . . .   — X X X —
(Appropriate basic symbol)

Fort . . . .

Fortified area . . . .

Fuel pipeline . . . .

Minefield . . . .

Airborne landing . . . .

The Arab-Israeli Wars

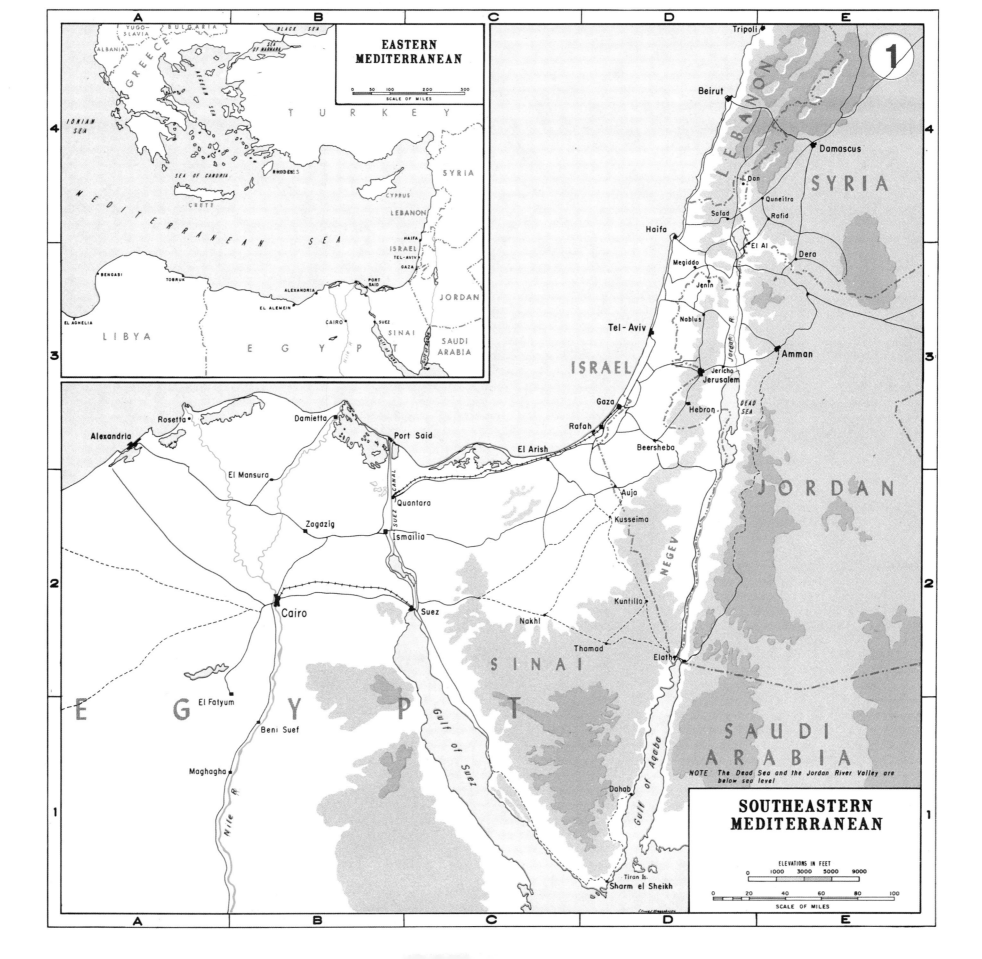

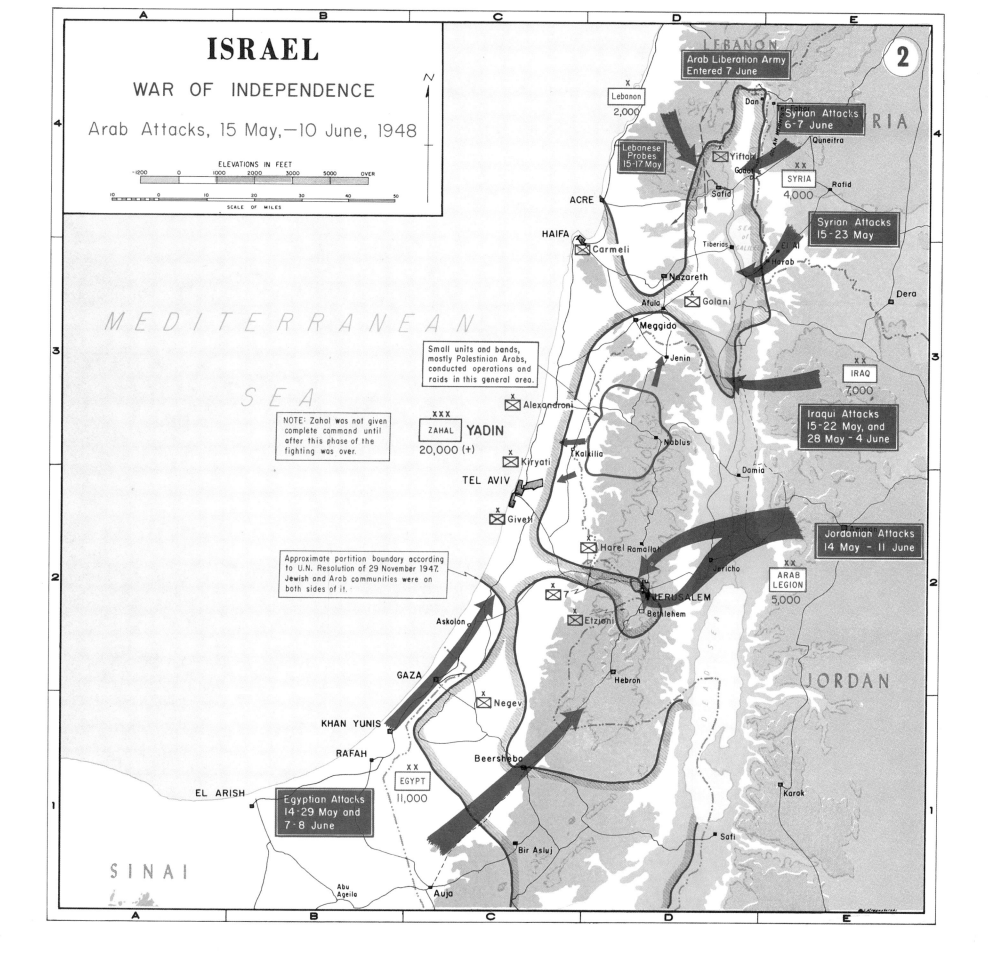

ISRAEL

WAR OF INDEPENDENCE

Arab Attacks, 15 May,—10 June, 1948

ELEVATIONS IN FEET

-1200   0   1000 2000 3000 5000 OVER

SCALE OF MILES

2

LEBANON

Arab Liberation Army
Entered 7 June

X
Lebanon
2,000

Dan

Syrian Attacks
6-7 June

RIA

Lebanese
Probes
15-17 May

X Yiftah

Quneitra

Gona

XX

SYRIA
4,000

Rafid

ACRE

HAIFA

Safid

Tiberias

El Al

Syrian Attacks
15-23 May

XX Carmeli

Harab

Dera

Nazareth

Afula

XX Golani

MEDITERRANEAN

Meggido

Jenin

Small units and bands,
mostly Palestinian Arabs,
conducted operations and
raids in this general area.

SEA

X Alexandroni

XXX

ZAHAL YADIN

20,000 (+)

NOTE: Zahal was not given
complete command until
after this phase of the
fighting was over.

Nablus

XX

IRAQ
7,000

Iraqui Attacks
15-22 May, and
28 May-4 June

XX Kiryati

Kalkilia

Damia

TEL AVIV

XX Givett

Amman

X Harel Ramallah

Jericho

Jordanian Attacks
14 May - 11 June

Approximate partition boundary according
to U.N. Resolution of 29 November 1947.
Jewish and Arab communities were on
both sides of it.

XX 7

JERUSALEM

XX

ARAB
LEGION
5,000

XX Etzioni

Bethlehem

Askolon

DEAD SEA

GAZA

Hebron

JORDAN

XX Negev

KHAN YUNIS

RAFAH

Beersheba

Karak

XX

EGYPT
11,000

EL ARISH

Egyptian Attacks
14-29 May and
7-8 June

Safi

SINAI

Bir Asluj

Abu
Ageila

Auja

ISRAEL

WAR OF INDEPENDENCE

October 1948 Battles

ELEVATIONS IN FEET

-1200   0   1000 2000 3000 5000 OVER

SCALE OF MILES

3

LEBANON

SYRIA

Arab
Liberation
Army
3,100

Arabs ithdrew
o Lebanon
30 October

Dan

Tel Fahar

Carmeli

Quneitra

Israeli Attacks
28-31 October

Oded

Godot
Nev

Rafid

ACRE

Safid

HAIFA

Golani   Tiberias

El Al

Harab

Nazareth

Dera

Afula

M E D I T E R R A N E A N

Meggido

Jenin

S E A

XXXX
ZAHAL YADIN
20,000 (?)

Kalkilia

Nablus

Damia

TEL AVIV

Brigade Oded arrived
19 October

Amman

Ramallah

Jericho

Approximate demarcation line
at the beginning of October

Oded   Harel

JERUSALEM

Givati

Bethlehem

Askolon

(+)

DEAD SEA

JORDAN

GAZA

Yiftach (+)

Hebron

KHAN YUNIS

Israeli Attacks
15-21 October

RAFAH

Beersheba

EGYPT
11,000(?)

Negev (-)

EL ARISH

Karak

Safi

S I N A I

Abu
Ageila

Auja

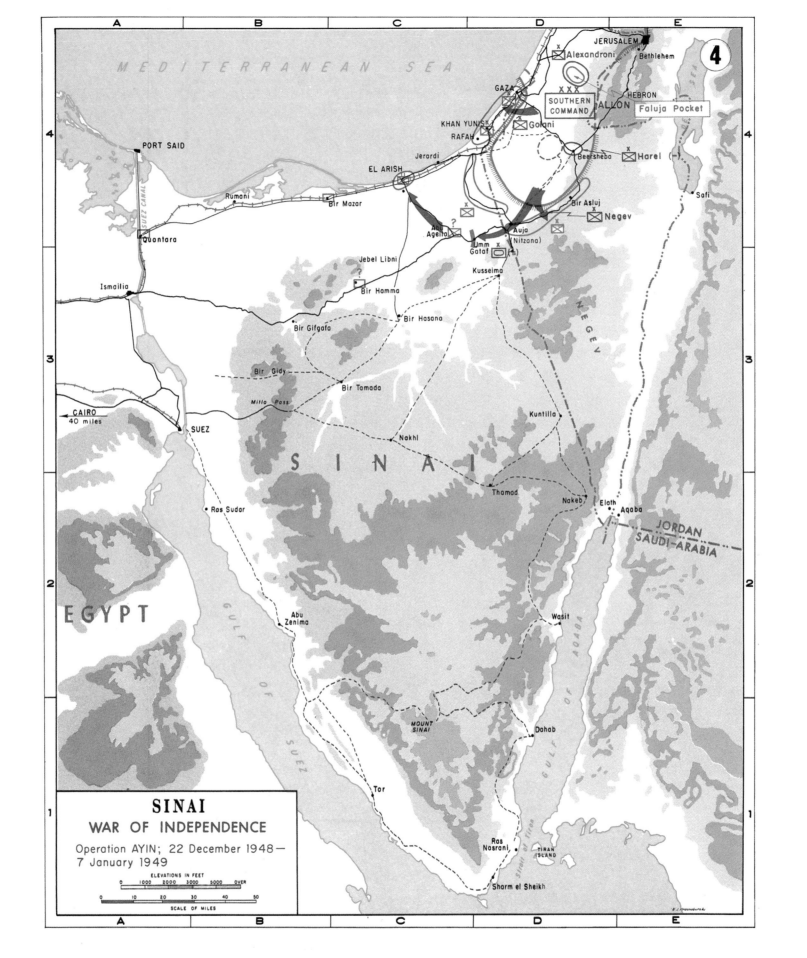

SINAI
WAR OF INDEPENDENCE
Operation AYIN; 22 December 1948—
7 January 1949

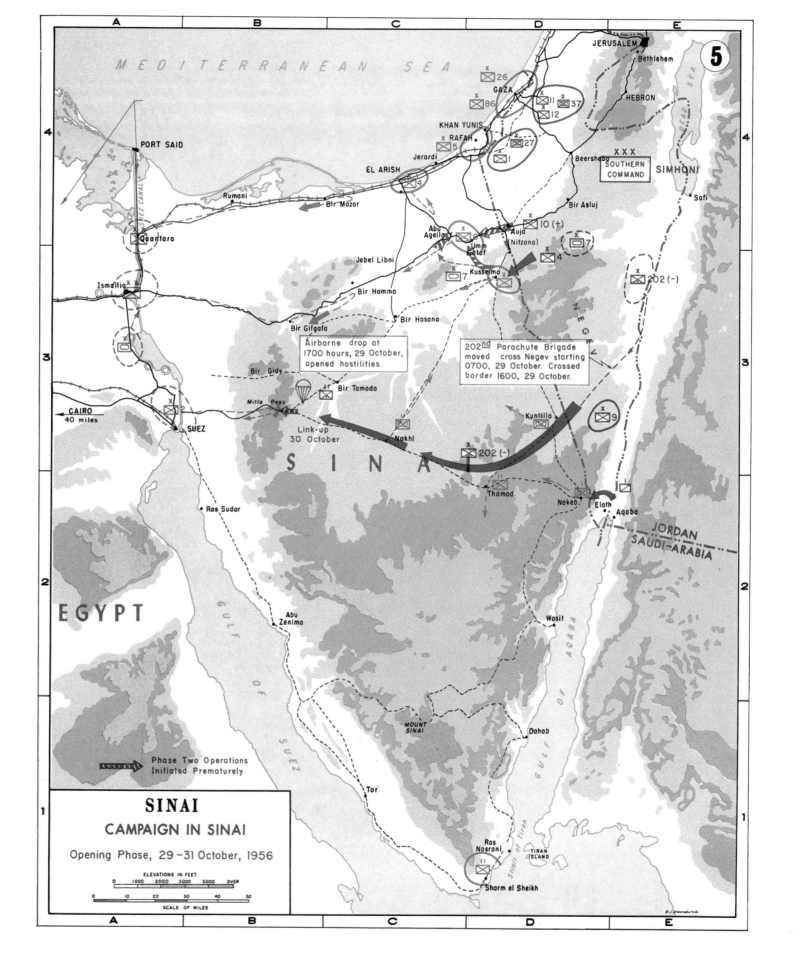

MEDITERRANEAN SEA

PORT SAID

GAZA

JERUSALEM

Bethlehem

HEBRON

KHAN YUNIS

RAFAH

Jerardi

EL ARISH

Beersheba

Rumani

Bir Mazar

SOUTHERN
COMMAND

SIMHONI

Safi

Quantara

Abu
Ageila

Auja
(Nitzana)

Bir Asluj

Umm
Gataf

Kusseima

Ismailia

Jebel Libni

NEGEV

Bir Hamma

Bir Gifgafa

Bir Hasana

202 (-)

Airborne drop at
1700 hours, 29 October,
opened hostilities.

202nd Parachute Brigade
moved cross Negev starting
0700, 29 October. Crossed
border 1600, 29 October.

Bir Gidy

Mitla Pass

Bir Tamada

Kuntilla

CAIRO
40 miles

SUEZ

Link-up
30 October

Nakhl

202 (-)

Thamad

Nakeb

Elath
Aqaba

JORDAN
SAUDI-ARABIA

Ras Sudar

EGYPT

Abu
Zenima

Wasit

GULF OF AQABA

GULF OF SUEZ

MOUNT
SINAI

Dahab

Phase Two Operations
Initiated Prematurely

SINAI

CAMPAIGN IN SINAI

Opening Phase, 29–31 October, 1956

Tor

Ras
Nasrani

Sharm el Sheikh

STRAIT OF TIRAN

TIRAN
ISLAND

ELEVATIONS IN FEET

1000 2000 3000 5000 OVER

0 10 20 30 40 50

SCALE OF MILES

S I N A I

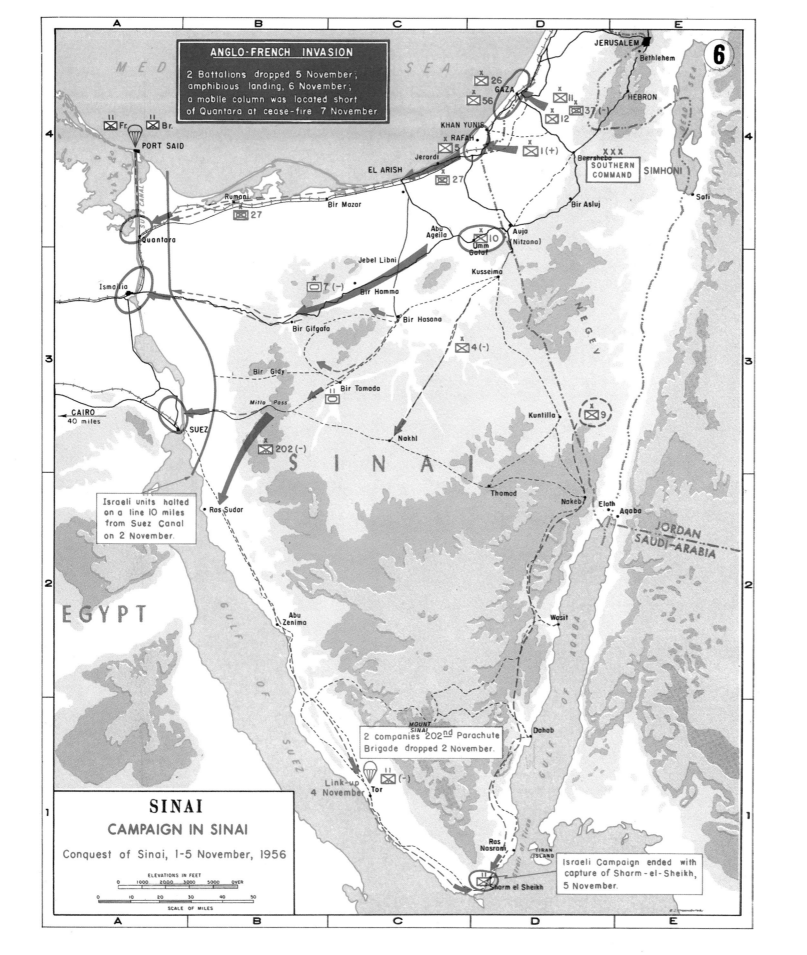

ANGLO-FRENCH INVASION

2 Battalions dropped 5 November;
amphibious landing, 6 November;
a mobile column was located short
of Quantara at cease-fire 7 November.

Israeli units halted
on a line 10 miles
from Suez Canal
on 2 November.

2 companies 202nd Parachute
Brigade dropped 2 November.

Link-up
4 November

Israeli Campaign ended with
capture of Sharm-el-Sheikh,
5 November.

SINAI

CAMPAIGN IN SINAI

Conquest of Sinai, 1-5 November, 1956

ELEVATIONS IN FEET

0   1000 2000 3000 5000 OVER

0   10   20   30   40   50

SCALE OF MILES

MEDITERRANEAN SEA

EGYPT

SINAI

NEGEV

JORDAN

SAUDI-ARABIA

JERUSALEM
Bethlehem
HEBRON
GAZA
KHAN YUNIS
RAFAH
Jerardi
EL ARISH
Beersheba
SOUTHERN COMMAND
SIMHONI
Bir Asluj
Safi
Rumani
Bir Mazar
Abu Ageila
Auja (Nitzana)
Umm Qataf
Jebel Libni
Kusseima
Quantara
Bir Homma
Ismailia
Bir Hasana
Bir Gifgafa
Bir Gidy
Bir Tamada
Mitla Pass
Kuntilla
CAIRO
40 miles
SUEZ
Nakhl
Ras Sudar
Thomad
Nakeb
Eloth
Aqaba
PORT SAID
Abu Zenima
Wasit
MOUNT SINAI
Dahab
Tor
Ras Nasrani
TIRAN ISLAND
Sharm el Sheikh

GULF OF SUEZ

GULF OF AQABA

6

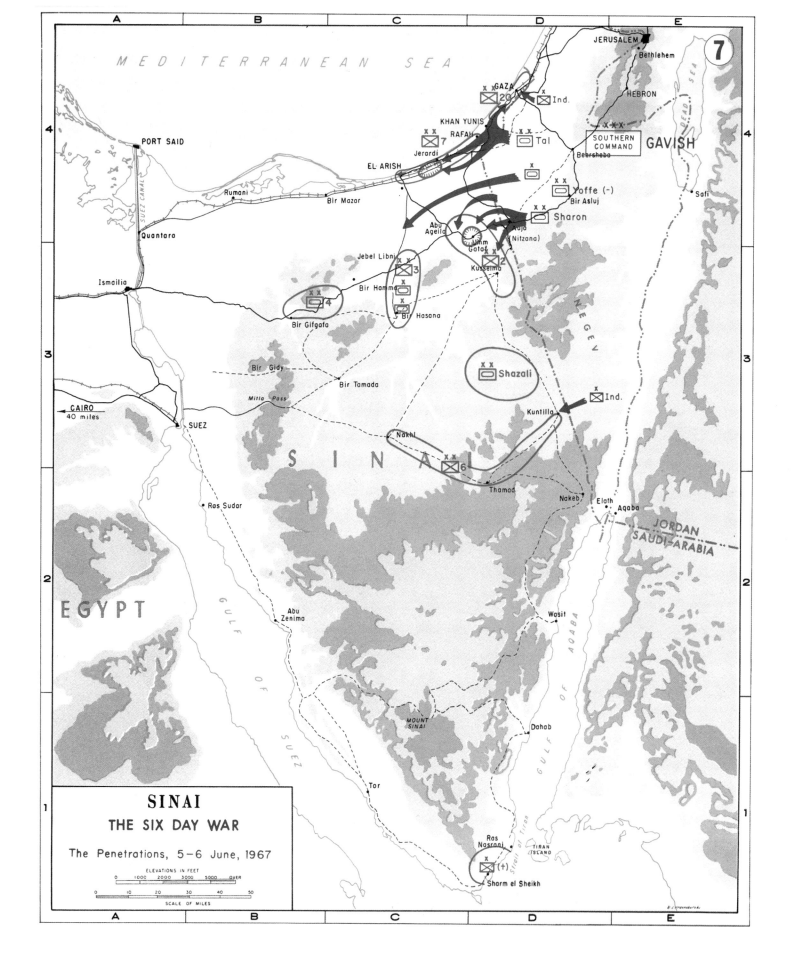

SINAI

THE SIX DAY WAR

The Penetrations, 5–6 June, 1967

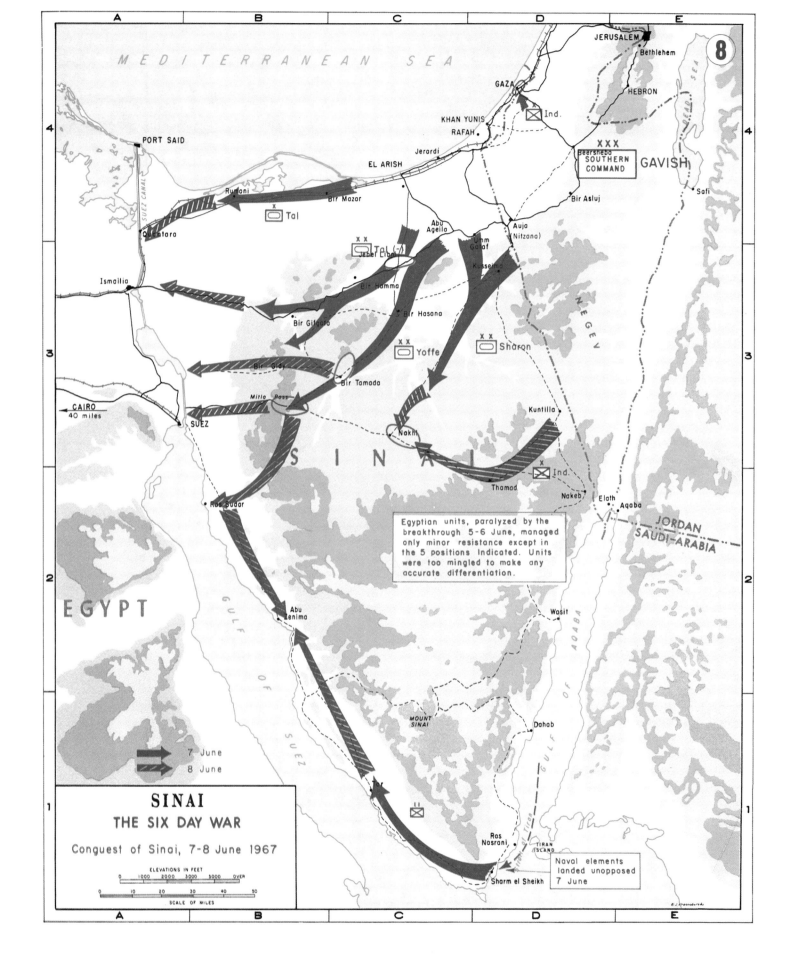

MEDITERRANEAN SEA

PORT SAID

EGYPT

CAIRO
40 miles

Egyptian units, paralyzed by the breakthrough 5-6 June, managed only minor resistance except in the 5 positions indicated. Units were too mingled to make any accurate differentiation.

JERUSALEM
Bethlehem
GAZA
HEBRON
KHAN YUNIS
RAFAH
Jerardi
Beersheba
SOUTHERN COMMAND GAVISH
EL ARISH
Bir Asluj
Safi
Rumani
Bir Mazar
Tal
Abu Ageila
Auja (Nitzana)
Qantara
Tel (-/)
Umm Gataf
Jebel Libni
Kusseima
Ismailia
Bir Hamma
N E G E V
Bir Gifgafa
Bir Hasana
Yoffe
Sharon
Bir Gidy
Bir Tamada
Mitla Pass
S I N A I
Kuntilla
SUEZ
Nakhl
Thamad
Nakeb
Ind.
Ras Sudar
Elath
Aqaba
JORDAN
SAUDI-ARABIA
Wasit
Abu Zenima
MOUNT SINAI
Dahab
GULF OF SUEZ
GULF OF AQABA
Ras Nasrani
TIRAN ISLAND

Naval elements landed unopposed 7 June

Sharm el Sheikh

7 June
8 June

SINAI
THE SIX DAY WAR
Conquest of Sinai, 7-8 June 1967

ELEVATIONS IN FEET
0   1000   2000   3000   4000   OVER

0   10   20   30   40   50
SCALE OF MILES

8

ISRAEL

THE SIX DAY WAR

The Jordan Salient, 5-7 June 1967

N

ELEVATIONS IN FEET

-1200   0   1000 2000 3000 5000 OVER

SCALE OF MILES

5-6 June
7 June

LEBANON

SYRIA

XXXX SYRIAN ARMY

Dan   Tel Fahar

Godot

Quneitra

Rofid

ACRE

Safid

XXX NORTHERN COMMAND ELAZAR

Tiberias   SEA of GALILEE   XX El Al

HAIFA

Horab

Nazareth

Dera

Afula

Meggido

MEDITERRANEAN

Jenin

SEA

Nablus

Kalkilia   XX

Damia

XXXX JORDANIAN ARMY HUSSEIN

ZAHAL RABIN

TEL AVIV

XXX CENTRAL COMMAND NARKIS

Ben-Ari

Ramallah   (+)   Jericho

Amman

JERUSALEM

Askolon

Bethlehem

GAZA

Hebron

DEAD SEA

JORDAN

KHAN YUNIS

RAFAH

Beersheba

XXX SOUTHERN COMMAND GAVISH

Karak

EL ARISH

SEE MAP 7; SITUATION ON THE SINAI FRONT ON 5 JUNE

Safi

SINAI

Bir Asluj

Abu Ageila   Auja

ISRAEL

THE SIX DAY WAR

Battle of Golan Heights, 9-10 June 1967

ELEVATIONS IN FEET

-1200 0 1000 2000 3000 5000 OVER

SCALE OF MILES

10 0 10 20 30 40 50

→ 9 June

⇢ 10 June

10

LEBANON

Dan Tel Fahar

GOLAN HEIGHTS

Qadas

Safid

SYRIA

SYRIAN ARMY

Quneitra

Rafid

ACRE

SEA of GALILEE

El Al

XXX NORTHERN COMMAND ELAZAR

Tiberias

HAIFA

Harab

Dera

Nazareth

Afula

Meggido

Jenin

MEDITERRANEAN

SEA

Nablus

XXXX ZAHAL RABIN

Kalkilia

Damia

TEL AVIV

XXXX JORDANIAN ARMY HUSSEIN

XXX CENTRAL COMMAND NARKIS

Ramallah

Amman

Jericho

JERUSALEM

Bethlehem

Askolon

DEAD SEA

JORDAN

GAZA

Hebron

KHAN YUNIS

RAFAH

Beersheba

Karak

EL ARISH

XXX SOUTHERN COMMAND GAVISH

Safi

Bir Asluj

SINAI

Abu Ageila

Auja

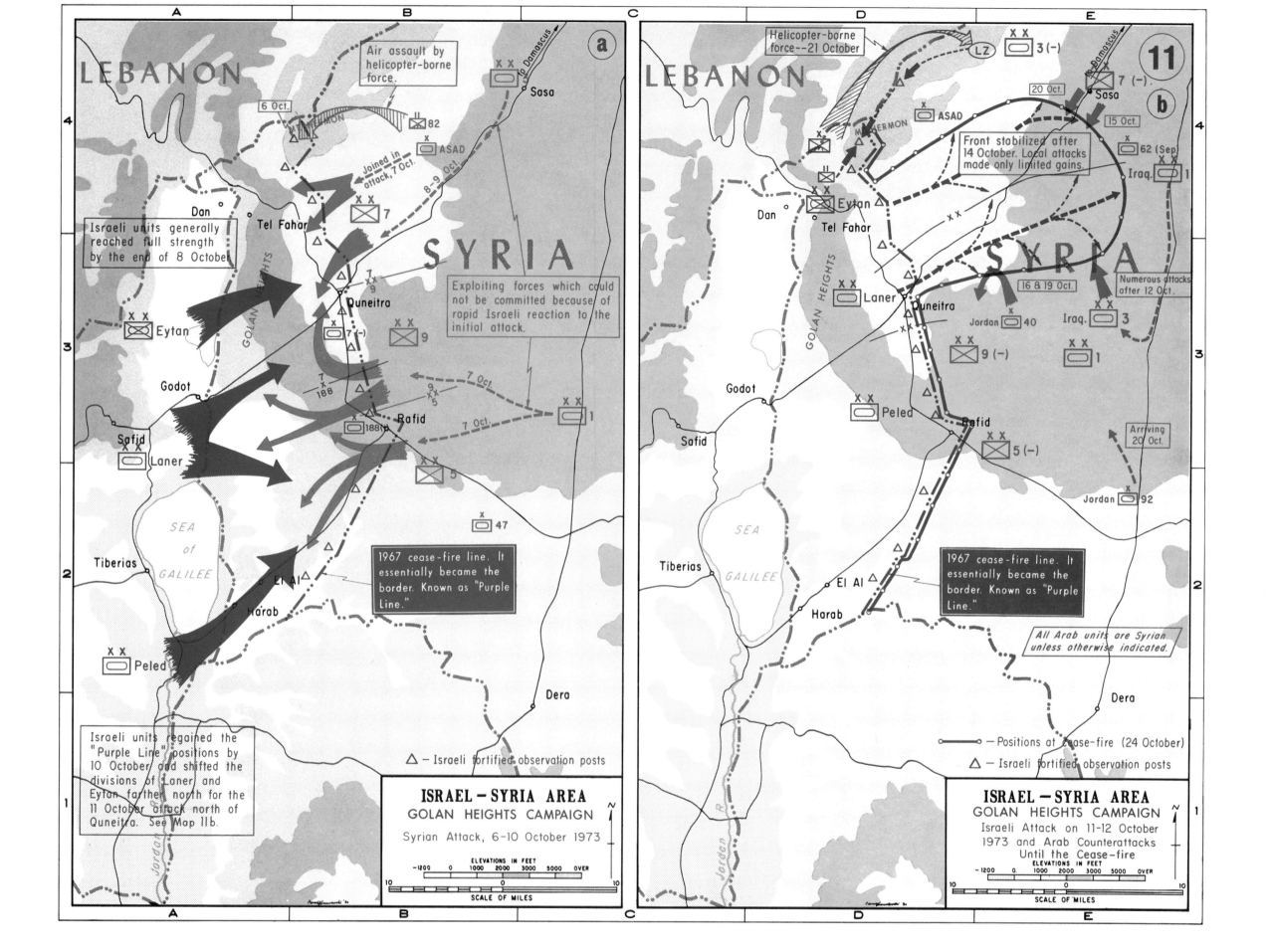

Map a:

LEBANON

SYRIA

Air assault by helicopter-borne force.

6 Oct.

82

ASAD

Joined in attack, 7 Oct.

8-9 Oct.

To Damascus

Sasa

XX

Dan

Tel Fahar

7

Israeli units generally reached full strength by the end of 8 October.

Eytan

XX

7
9

Quneitra

7 (-)

9

Exploiting forces which could not be committed because of rapid Israeli reaction to the initial attack.

Godot

7
188

7 Oct.

9
5

7 Oct.

1

Safid

Laner

188

Rafid

7 Oct.

5

SEA of GALILEE

47

1967 cease-fire line. It essentially became the border. Known as "Purple Line."

Tiberias

El Al

Harab

Peled

Israeli units regained the "Purple Line" positions by 10 October and shifted the divisions of Laner and Eytan farther north for the 11 October attack north of Quneitra. See Map 11b.

Dera

△ – Israeli fortified observation posts

ISRAEL – SYRIA AREA
GOLAN HEIGHTS CAMPAIGN

Syrian Attack, 6-10 October 1973

ELEVATIONS IN FEET
-1200 0 1000 2000 3000 5000 OVER

SCALE OF MILES
10 0 10

Map b:

Helicopter-borne force--21 October

LEBANON

LZ

3 (-)

To Damascus

20 Oct.

ASAD

7 (-)

Sasa

15 Oct.

Front stabilized after 14 October. Local attacks made only limited gains.

XX

Dan

Eytan

Tel Fahar

62 (Sep)

Iraq. 1

SYRIA

16 & 19 Oct.

Numerous attacks after 12 October.

Laner

XX

Quneitra

Jordan 40

Iraq. 3

Godot

9 (-)

1

Peled

Rafid

Arriving 20 Oct.

Safid

5 (-)

SEA GALILEE

Jordan 92

1967 cease-fire line. It essentially became the border. Known as "Purple Line."

Tiberias

El Al

Harab

All Arab units are Syrian unless otherwise indicated.

Dera

○—○ – Positions at Cease-fire (24 October)
△ – Israeli fortified observation posts

ISRAEL – SYRIA AREA
GOLAN HEIGHTS CAMPAIGN

Israeli Attack on 11-12 October 1973 and Arab Counterattacks Until the Cease-fire

ELEVATIONS IN FEET
-1200 0 1000 2000 3000 5000 OVER

SCALE OF MILES
10 0 10

11

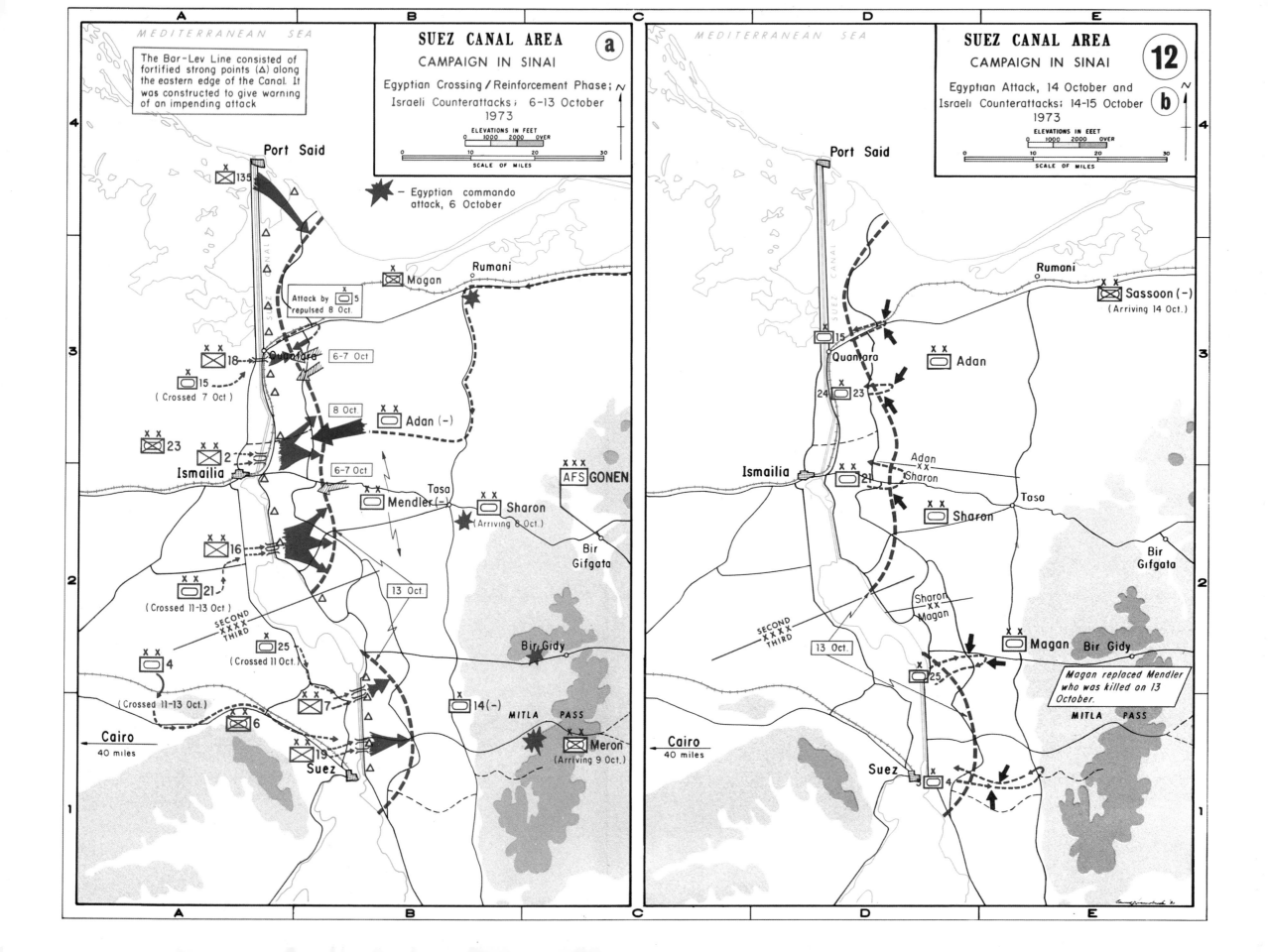

SUEZ CANAL AREA
CAMPAIGN IN SINAI

(a)

Egyptian Crossing / Reinforcement Phase;
Israeli Counterattacks; 6-13 October
1973

ELEVATIONS IN FEET
0 1000 2000 OVER
0   10   20   30
SCALE OF MILES

The Bar-Lev Line consisted of fortified strong points (△) along the eastern edge of the Canal. It was constructed to give warning of an impending attack

✦ — Egyptian commando attack, 6 October

SUEZ CANAL AREA
CAMPAIGN IN SINAI

(12)
(b)

Egyptian Attack, 14 October and
Israeli Counterattacks; 14-15 October
1973

ELEVATIONS IN FEET
0 1000 2000 OVER
0   10   20   30
SCALE OF MILES

MEDITERRANEAN SEA

Port Said

135

Magan

Rumani

Attack by 5 repulsed 8 Oct.

18 Quantara 6-7 Oct

15 (Crossed 7 Oct)

8 Oct.

Adan (-)

23

2 6-7 Oct

Ismailia

Tasa

AFS GONEN

Mendler (=)

Sharon (Arriving 8 Oct.)

16

Bir Gifgata

21 (Crossed 11-13 Oct.)

SECOND THIRD

13 Oct.

Bir Gidy

25 (Crossed 11 Oct.)

4

14 (-)

MITLA PASS

Cairo 40 miles

(Crossed 11-13 Oct.)

7

6

19 Suez

Meron (Arriving 9 Oct.)

MEDITERRANEAN SEA

Port Said

Rumani

Sassoon (-) (Arriving 14 Oct.)

15 Quantara

Adan

24 23

Ismailia

21

Adan Sharon

Sharon

Tasa

Sharon Magan

Magan Bir Gidy

SECOND THIRD

13 Oct.

25

Magan replaced Mendler who was killed on 13 October.

MITLA PASS

Cairo 40 miles

Suez 5 4

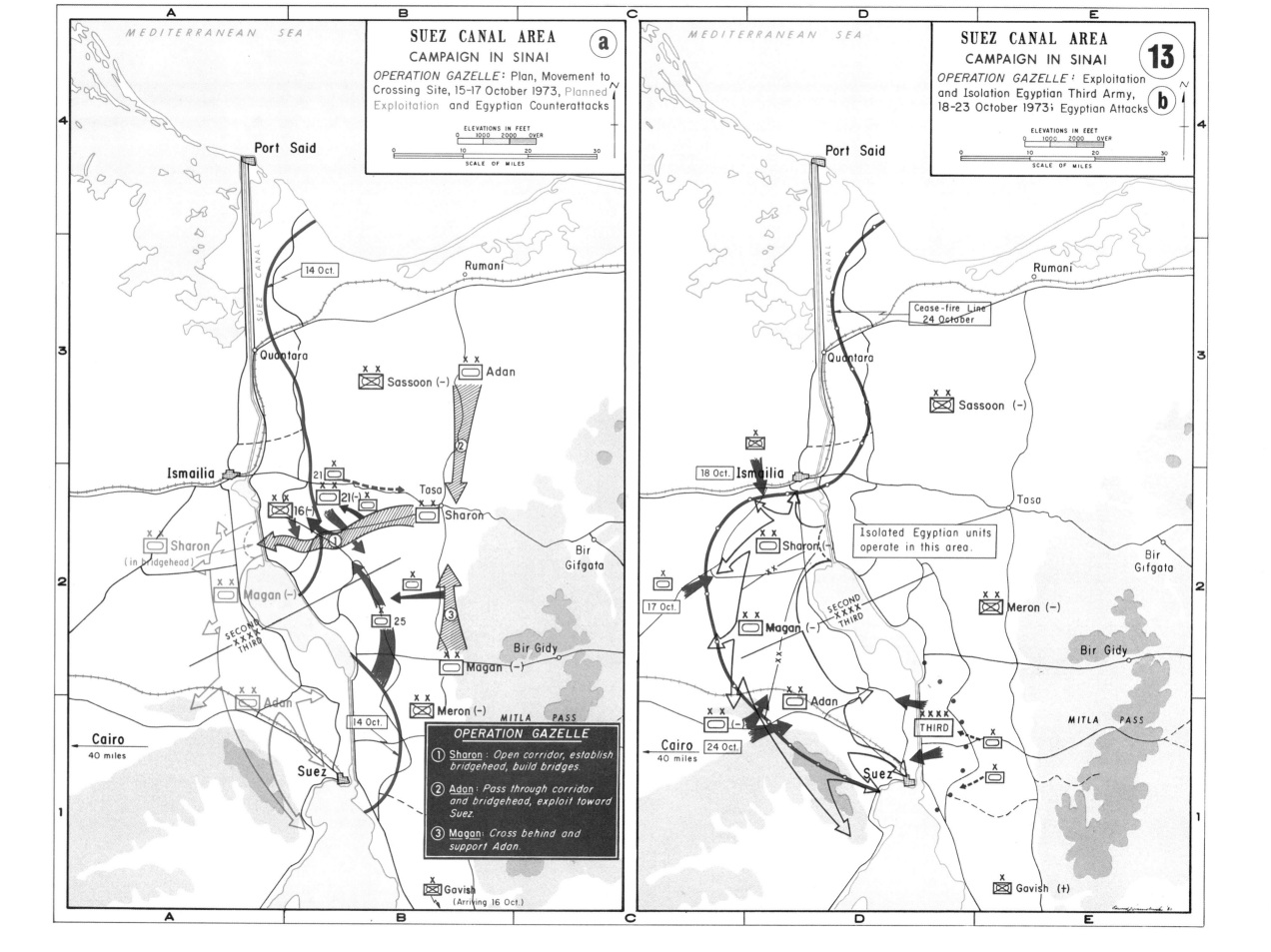

Map a (left panel)

MEDITERRANEAN SEA

SUEZ CANAL AREA
CAMPAIGN IN SINAI

a

OPERATION GAZELLE: Plan, Movement to
Crossing Site, 15-17 October 1973, Planned
Exploitation and Egyptian Counterattacks

ELEVATIONS IN FEET
1000 2000 OVER
0   10   20   30
SCALE OF MILES

Port Said

14 Oct.

Rumani

SUEZ CANAL

Quantara

Sassoon (-)

Adan

②

Ismailia

21

21(-)

Tasa

16(-)

Sharon

①

Sharon
(in bridgehead)

Bir
Gifgata

Magan (-)

25

③

SECOND
XXXX
THIRD

Adan

Magan (-)

Bir Gidy

14 Oct.

Meron (-)

MITLA PASS

Cairo
40 miles

Suez

OPERATION GAZELLE

① <u>Sharon</u>: *Open corridor, establish
bridgehead, build bridges.*

② <u>Adan</u>: *Pass through corridor
and bridgehead, exploit toward
Suez.*

③ <u>Magan</u>: *Cross behind and
support Adan.*

Gavish
(Arriving 16 Oct.)

Map b (right panel)

MEDITERRANEAN SEA

SUEZ CANAL AREA
CAMPAIGN IN SINAI

13

OPERATION GAZELLE: Exploitation
and Isolation Egyptian Third Army,
18-23 October 1973; Egyptian Attacks

b

ELEVATIONS IN FEET
1000 2000 OVER
0   10   20   30
SCALE OF MILES

Port Said

SUEZ CANAL

Rumani

Cease-fire Line
24 October

Quantara

Sassoon (-)

18 Oct. Ismailia

Tasa

Sharon (-)

Isolated Egyptian units
operate in this area.

Bir
Gifgata

17 Oct.

SECOND
XXXX
THIRD

Meron (-)

Magan (-)

Bir Gidy

Adan

(-)

THIRD

MITLA PASS

Cairo
40 miles

24 Oct.

Suez

Gavish (+)

The Chinese Civil War

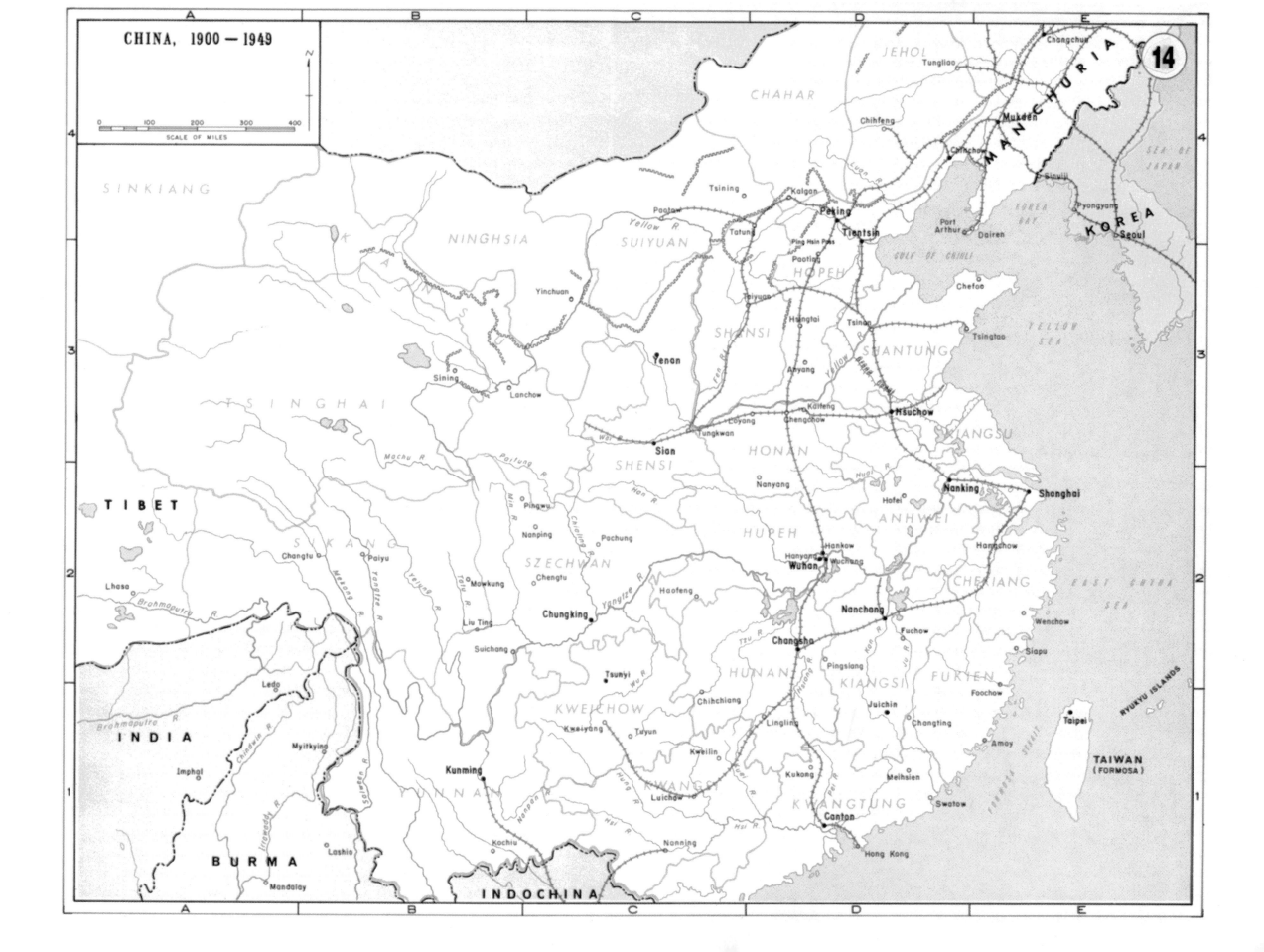

CHINA, 1900 — 1949

N

0   100   200   300   400
SCALE OF MILES

14

SINKIANG

JEHOL

CHAHAR

MANCHURIA

Changchun

Tungliao

Chihfeng

Mukden

SEA OF JAPAN

Chinchow

Tsining

Kalgan

Sinuiji

KOREA BAY

Paotow

Peking

Pyongyang

Tatung

Tientsin

KOREA

NINGHSIA

SUIYUAN

Ping Hsin Pass

Port Arthur

Dairen

Seoul

Yellow R

Paoting

HOPEH

GULF OF CHIHLI

Yinchuan

Taiyuan

Chefoo

K

Hangtai

Tsinan

SHENSI

SHANTUNG

Tsingtao

YELLOW SEA

Yenan

Anyang

Sining

Lanchow

Yellow R

Grand Canal

Kaifeng

Hsuchow

Loyang

Chengchow

KIANGSU

Machu R

Wei R

Tungkwan

TSINGHAI

Paitung R

Sian

HONAN

Han R

Nanyang

Hwai R

Nanking

Shanghai

TIBET

Min R

Pingwu

SHENSI

Hofei

ANHWEI

Chiaki

Han R

Nanping

Pachung

HUPEH

Hankow

Hangchow

SIKANG

Mekong R

Yangtze R

Salween R

Mowkung

Chengtu

Hanyang

Wuchang

CHEKIANG

Changtu

Paiyu

Tatu R

SZECHWAN

Wuhan

EAST CHINA SEA

Lhasa

Brahmaputra R

Haofeng

Yangtze R

Liu Ting

Chungking

Nanchang

Wenchow

Brahmaputra R

Tzu R

Changsha

Fuchow

Siapu

Suichang

Fen R

HUNAN

Pingsiang

Kan R

KIANGSI

FUKIEN

INDIA

Chindwin R

Tsunyi

Wu R

Chihchiang

Lingling

Juichin

Foochow

Ledo

KWEICHOW

Hsiang R

Changting

Imphal

Kwangsi

Kweilin

Kukong

Meihsien

Taipei

Myitkyina

Kweiyang

Tuyun

RYUKYU ISLANDS

Irrawaddy R

Kweichow

KWANGSI

Kuei R

Amoy

TAIWAN (FORMOSA)

Kunming

Luichow To

Swatow

YUNNAN

Hung R

KWANGTUNG

Lashio

Kochiu

Nanpan R

Nanning

Canton

FORMOSA STRAIT

BURMA

Hsi R

Hong Kong

Mandalay

INDOCHINA

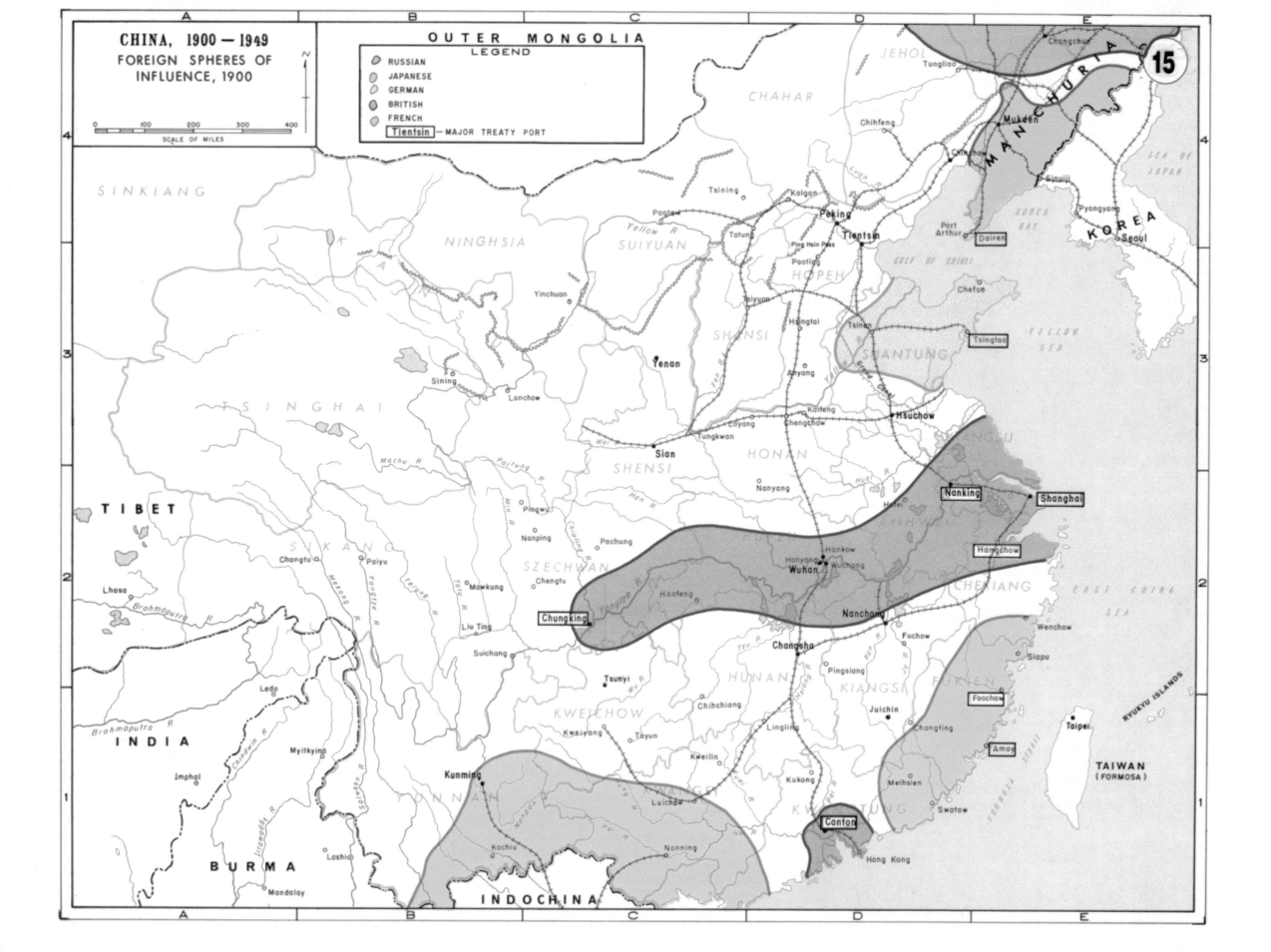

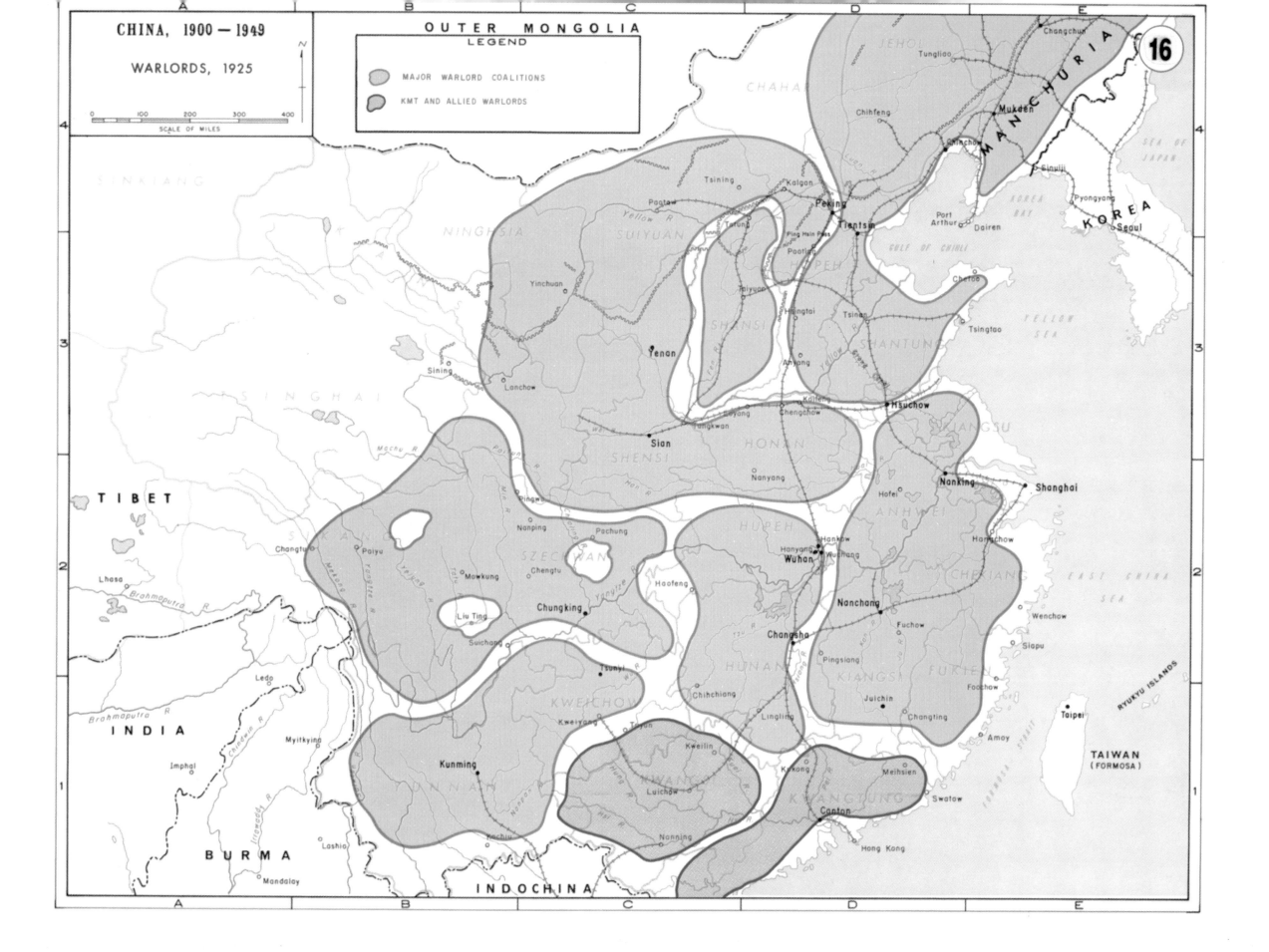

CHINA, 1900 — 1949

WARLORDS, 1925

N

SCALE OF MILES
0   100   200   300   400

OUTER MONGOLIA

LEGEND

MAJOR WARLORD COALITIONS

KMT AND ALLIED WARLORDS

16

MANCHURIA

Changchun

JEHOL

Tungliao

CHAHAR

Chihfeng

Mukden

Kalgan

Peking

Chinchow

Sinuiji

KOREA

Paotow

Ping Hsin Pass

Tientsin

Port Arthur   Dairen

Pyongyang

Seoul

SUIYUAN

Tatung

Paoting

GULF OF CHILI

KOREA BAY

NINGHSIA

Yinchuan

Taiyuan

Hsingtai

Tsinan

Chefoo

SEA OF JAPAN

Tsining

SINKIANG

Sining

Lanchow

Yenan

SHENSI

Anyang

SHANTUNG

Tsingtao

YELLOW SEA

TSINGHAI

Kaifeng

Loyang   Chengchow

Hsuchow

KIANGSU

Tungkwan

Sian

HONAN

Mochu R.

SHENSI

Nanyang

Hofei

Nanking

Shanghai

TIBET

Lhasa

Brahmaputra R.

Pingwu

Nanping

Pachung

HUPEH

Hankow

Hanyang   Wuchang

Wuhan

ANHWEI

Hangchow

CHEKIANG

EAST CHINA SEA

Changtu

Paiyu

SZECHWAN

Mowkung

Chengtu

Haofeng

SIKANG

Liu Ting

Chungking

Nanchang

Fuchow

Wenchow

Suichang

Changsha

KIANGSI

Siapu

INDIA

Ledo

Tsunyi

Chihchiang

HUNAN

Pingsiang

Juichin

Foochow

Imphal

Myitkyina

KWEICHOW

Kweiyang

Tsjan

Lingling

Kukong

Changting

Amoy

Taipei

RYUKYU ISLANDS

BURMA

Lashio

Kunming

YUNNAN

Kweilin

KWANGSI

Luichow

KWANGTUNG

Meihsien

Swatow

Canton

TAIWAN
(FORMOSA)

Mandalay

Kochiu

Nanning

Hong Kong

INDOCHINA

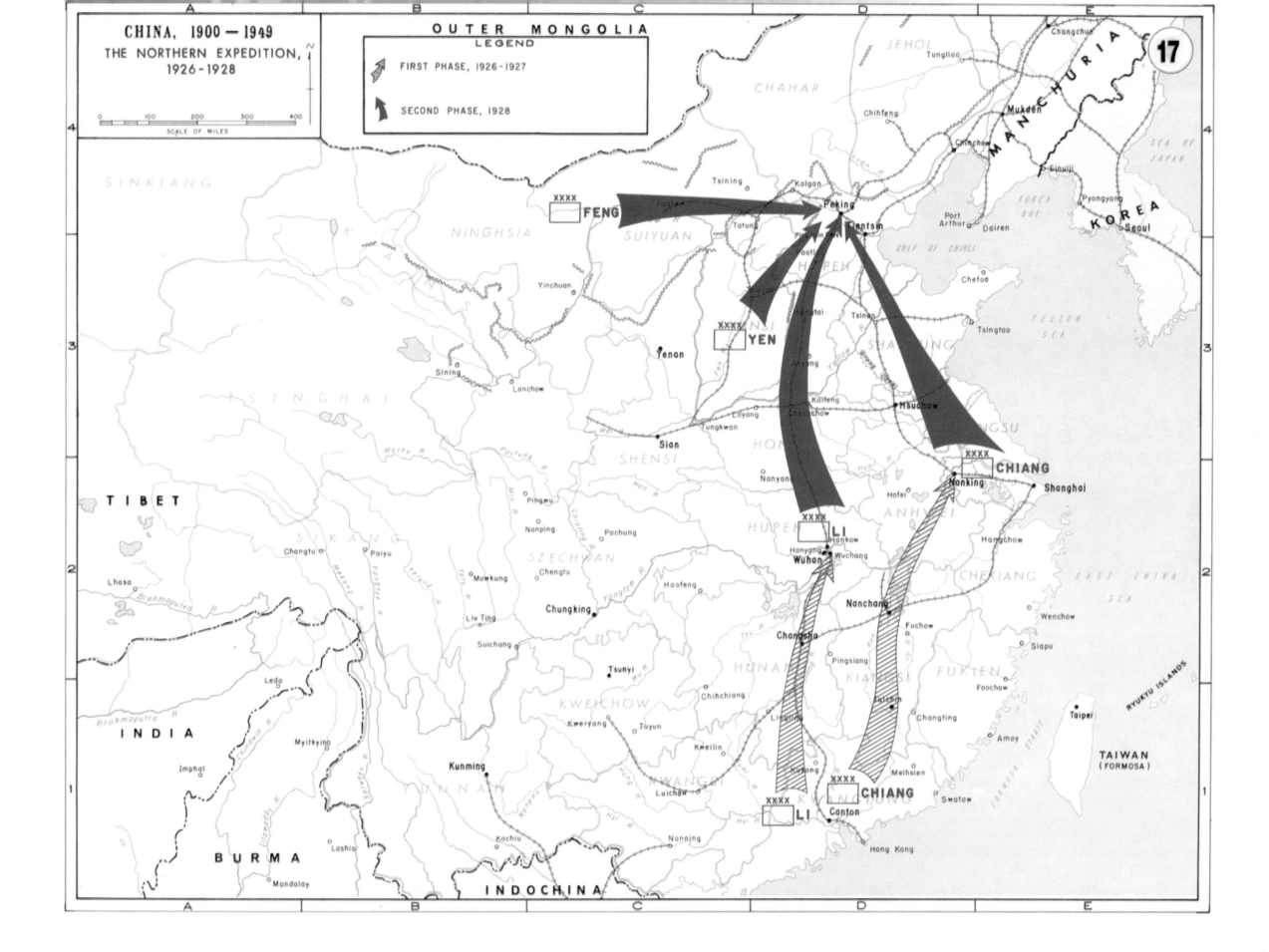

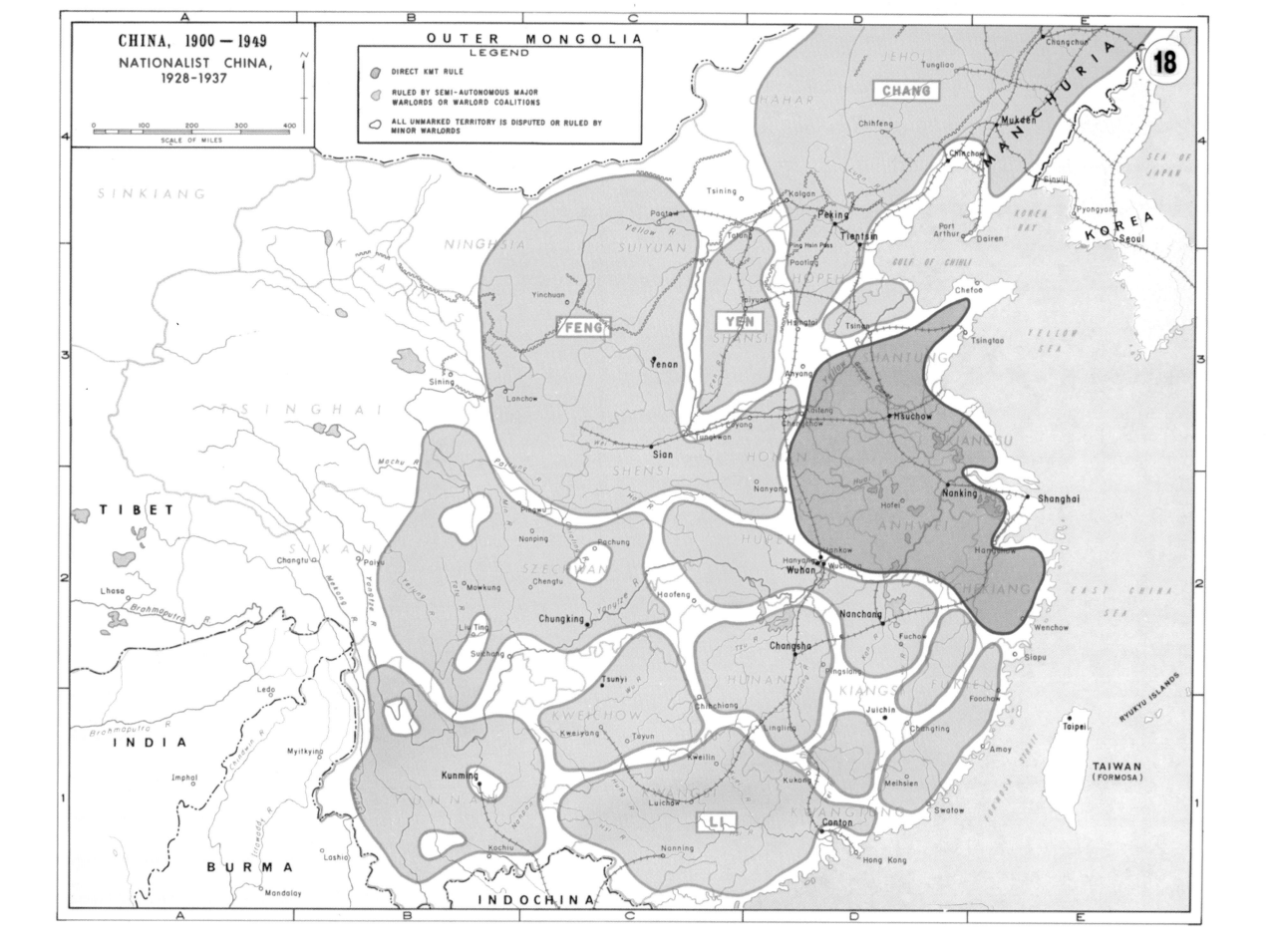

CHINA, 1900 — 1949
NATIONALIST CHINA, 1928-1937

OUTER MONGOLIA

LEGEND

- DIRECT KMT RULE
- RULED BY SEMI-AUTONOMOUS MAJOR WARLORDS OR WARLORD COALITIONS
- ALL UNMARKED TERRITORY IS DISPUTED OR RULED BY MINOR WARLORDS

N

SCALE OF MILES
0   100   200   300   400

18

SINKIANG

CHAHAR

JEHOL

CHANG

MANCHURIA

Changchun

Tungliao

Chihfeng

Mukden

Chinchow

Sinuiji

SEA OF JAPAN

KOREA

Pyongyang

Seoul

Tsining

Kalgan

Peking

Port Arthur

Dairen

KOREA BAY

Paotow

Yellow R

Tatung

Tientsin

Ping Hsin Pass

Paoting

GULF OF CHIHLI

NINGHSIA

SUIYUAN

HOPEH

Chefoo

FENG

Yinchuan

Taiyuan

YEN

Hsingtai

Tsinan

Tsingtao

YELLOW SEA

SHENSI

SHANTUNG

Yenan

Ahyang

Yellow R

Sining

Lanchow

Kaifeng

Chengchow

Hsuchow

KIANGSU

TSINGHAI

Loyang

Tungkwan

HONAN

TIBET

Wei R

Sian

Nanyang

Hwai R

Hofei

Nanking

Shanghai

Machu R

Paitung R

SHENSI

Hangchow

Lhasa

Brahmaputra

SIKANG

Changtu

Paiyu

Pingwu

Nanping

Pachung

ANHWEI

HUPEH

CHEKIANG

Mekong R

Yalung R

Chialing R

Hanyang

Hankow

Wuchang

Nanchang R

Nanchang R

SZECHWAN

Chengtu

Wuhan

EAST CHINA SEA

INDIA

Brahmaputra R

Keiyang R

Tatu R

Mowkung

Haofeng

Yangtze R

Nanchang

Wenchow

Ledo

Liu Ting

Chungking

Fuchow

Imphal

Chindwin R

Suichang

Yangtze R

Changsha

KIANGSI

FUKIEN

Siapu

Myitkyina

Tsunyi

Wu R

HUNAN

Pingsiang

Kan R

Juichin

Foochow

LI

KWEICHOW

Chinchiang

Hsiang R

Changting

Lashio

Kweiyang

Tayun

Lingling

Kukong

Amoy

Kunming

YUNNAN

Kweilin

TAIWAN
(FORMOSA)

Taipei

RYUKYU ISLANDS

BURMA

Kochiu

Luichow

KWANGSI

Kukong

KWANGTUNG

Swatow

Meihsien

Mandalay

INDOCHINA

Hsi R

Nanning

Canton

Hong Kong

FORMOSA STRAIT

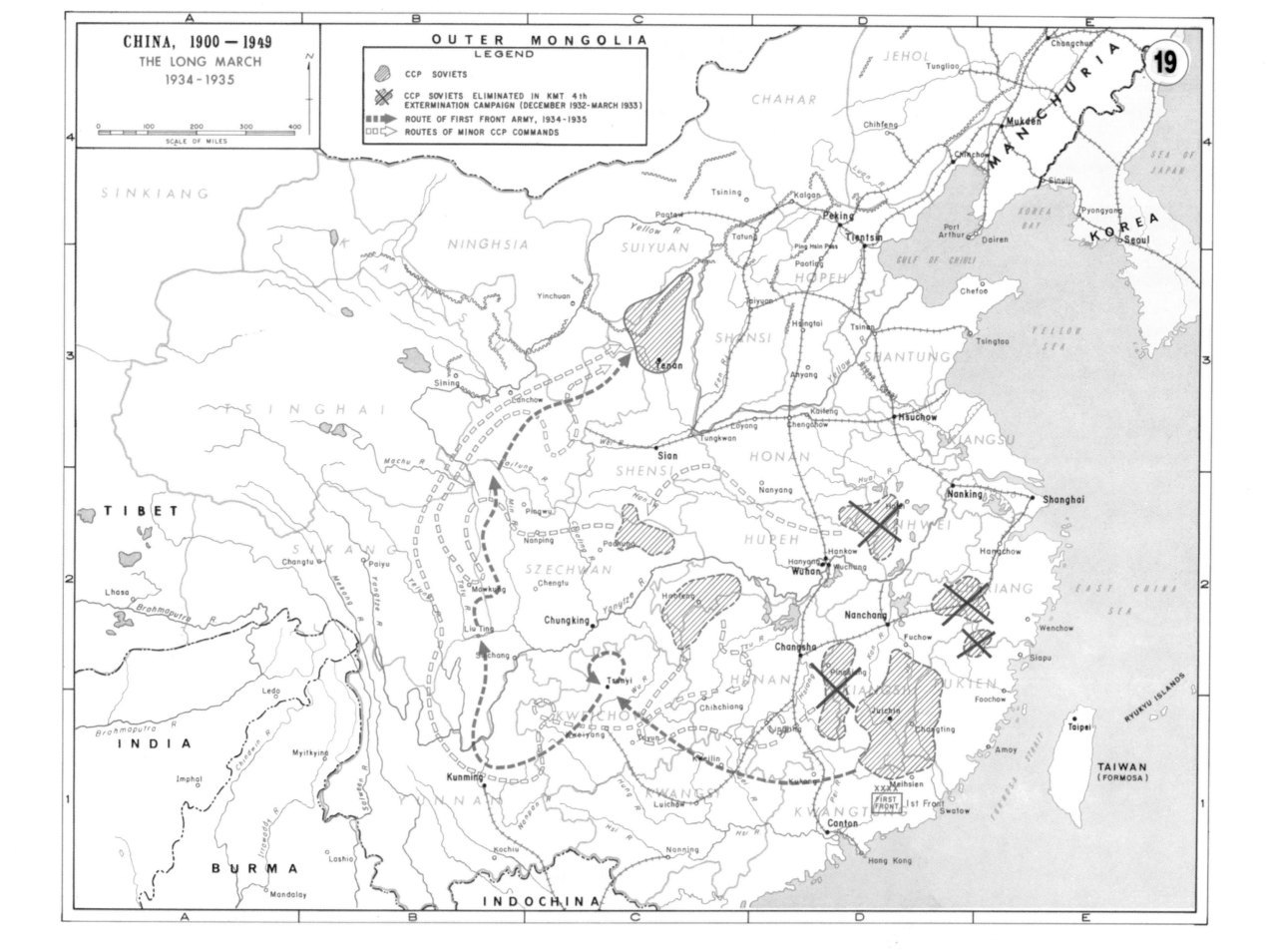

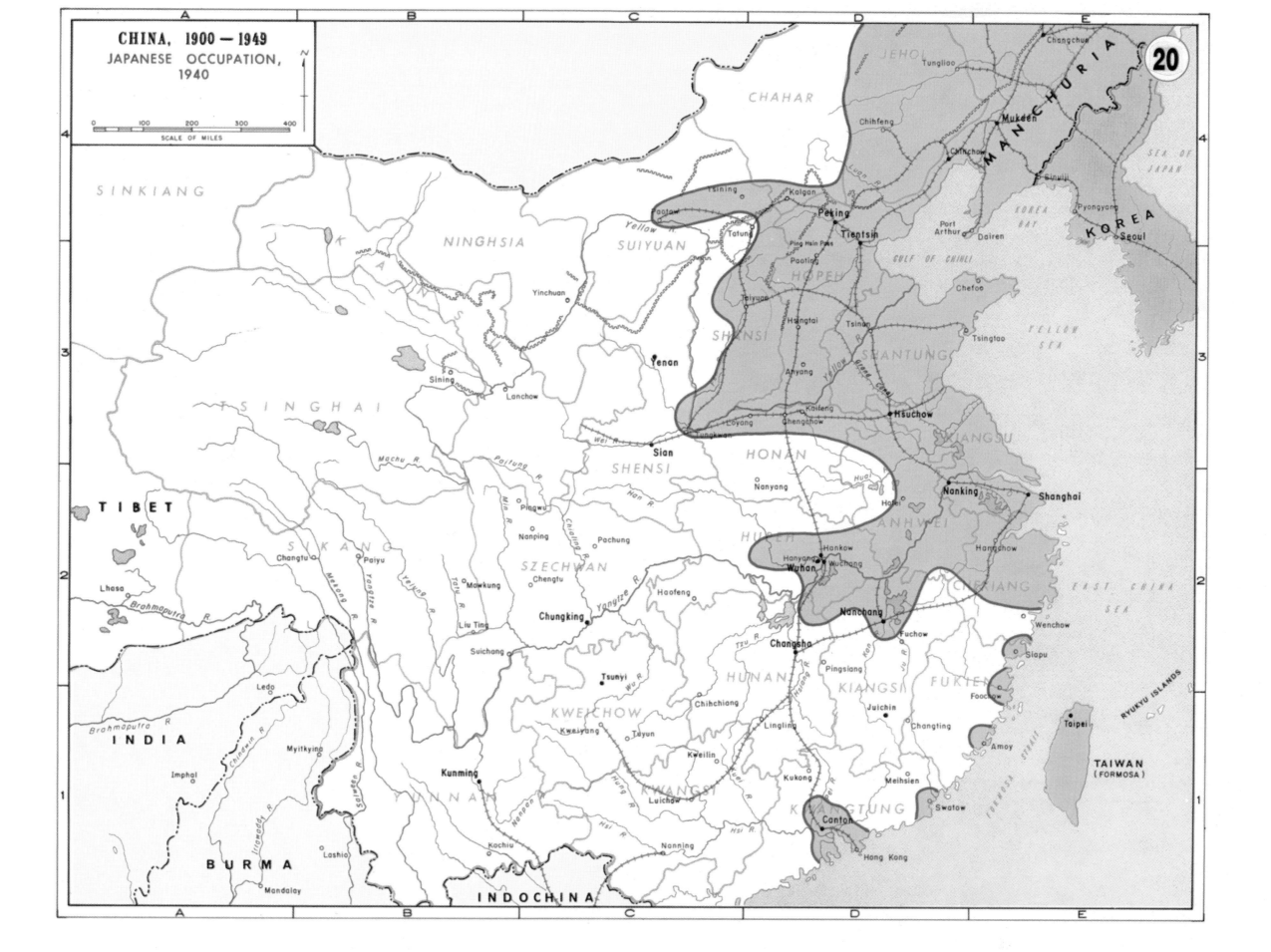

CHINA, 1900 — 1949
JAPANESE OCCUPATION, 1940

SCALE OF MILES
0   100   200   300   400

20

SINKIANG

CHAHAR

MANCHURIA

Changchun

Tungliao

Chihfeng

Mukden

Chinchow

Sinuiji

SEA OF JAPAN

NINGHSIA

SUIYUAN

Yellow R.

Tsining

Paotow

Kalgan

Tatung

Peking

Tientsin

Ping Hsin Pass

Paoting

KOREA BAY

Port Arthur

Dairen

Pyongyang

KOREA

Seoul

HOPEH

GULF OF CHIHLI

Chefoo

Yinchuan

Taiyuan

Hsingtai

Tsinan

SHENSI

SHANTUNG

Tsingtao

YELLOW SEA

Yenan

Anyang

Yellow R.

Grand Canal

Sining

Lanchow

TSINGHAI

Kaifeng

Hsuchow

KIANGSU

Loyang

Chengchow

Tungkwan

Wei R.

Machu R.

Paitung R.

Sian

HONAN

Hwai R.

TIBET

SHENSI

Nanyang

Han R.

Hofei

Nanking

Shanghai

Lhasa

Brahmaputra R.

SIKANG

Mekong R.

Yangtze R.

Min R.

Pingwu

Nanping

Pachung

Chialing R.

ANHWEI

Hanyang Hankow
Wuchang

Wuhan

Hangchow

Changtu

Paiyu

SZECHWAN

Chengtu

Mowkung

Tatu R.

Haofeng

HUPEH

CHEKIANG

EAST CHINA SEA

Yangtze R.

Nanchang

Yalung R.

Liu Ting

Chungking

Suichang

Changsha

Fuchow

Wenchow

Brahmaputra R.

Chindwin R.

INDIA

Ledo

Myitkyina

Imphal

Tsunyi

Wu R.

KWEICHOW

Chihchiang

HUNAN

Tzu R.

Pingsiang

Kan R.

KIANGSI

Yu R.

Siapu

FUKIEN

Kweiyang

Tayun

Lingling

Juichin

Foochow

Kweilin

Changting

Meihsien

Amoy

FORMOSA STRAIT

Taipei

RYUKYU ISLANDS

Kunming

YUNNAN

Nanpan R.

KWANGSI

Luichow

Hsiang R.

Kukong

Yuen R.

Hsi R.

KWANGTUNG

Swatow

TAIWAN (FORMOSA)

Lashio

Salween R.

Kochiu

Hsi R.

Nanning

Canton

Hong Kong

Irrawaddy R.

BURMA

INDOCHINA

Mandalay

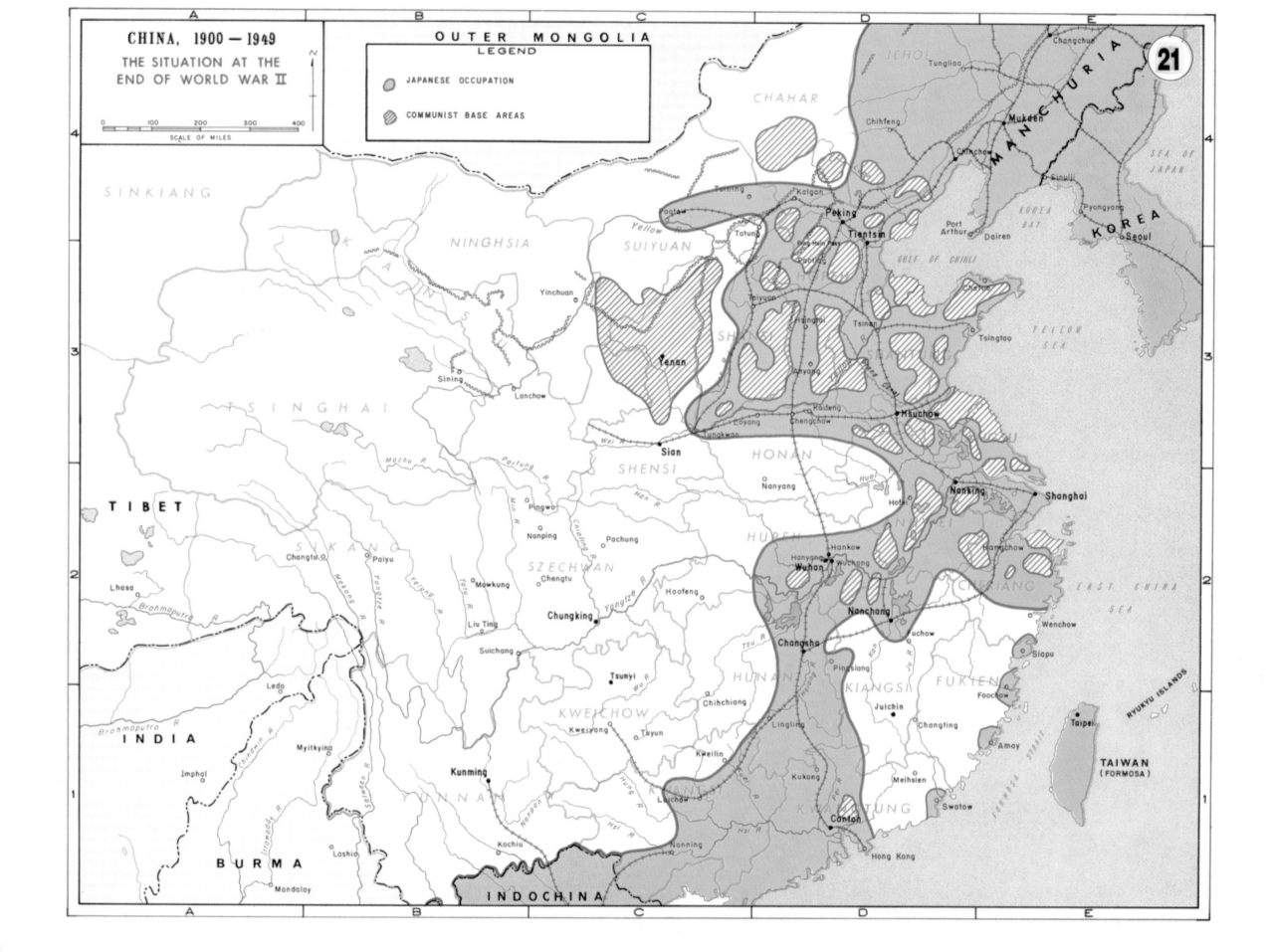

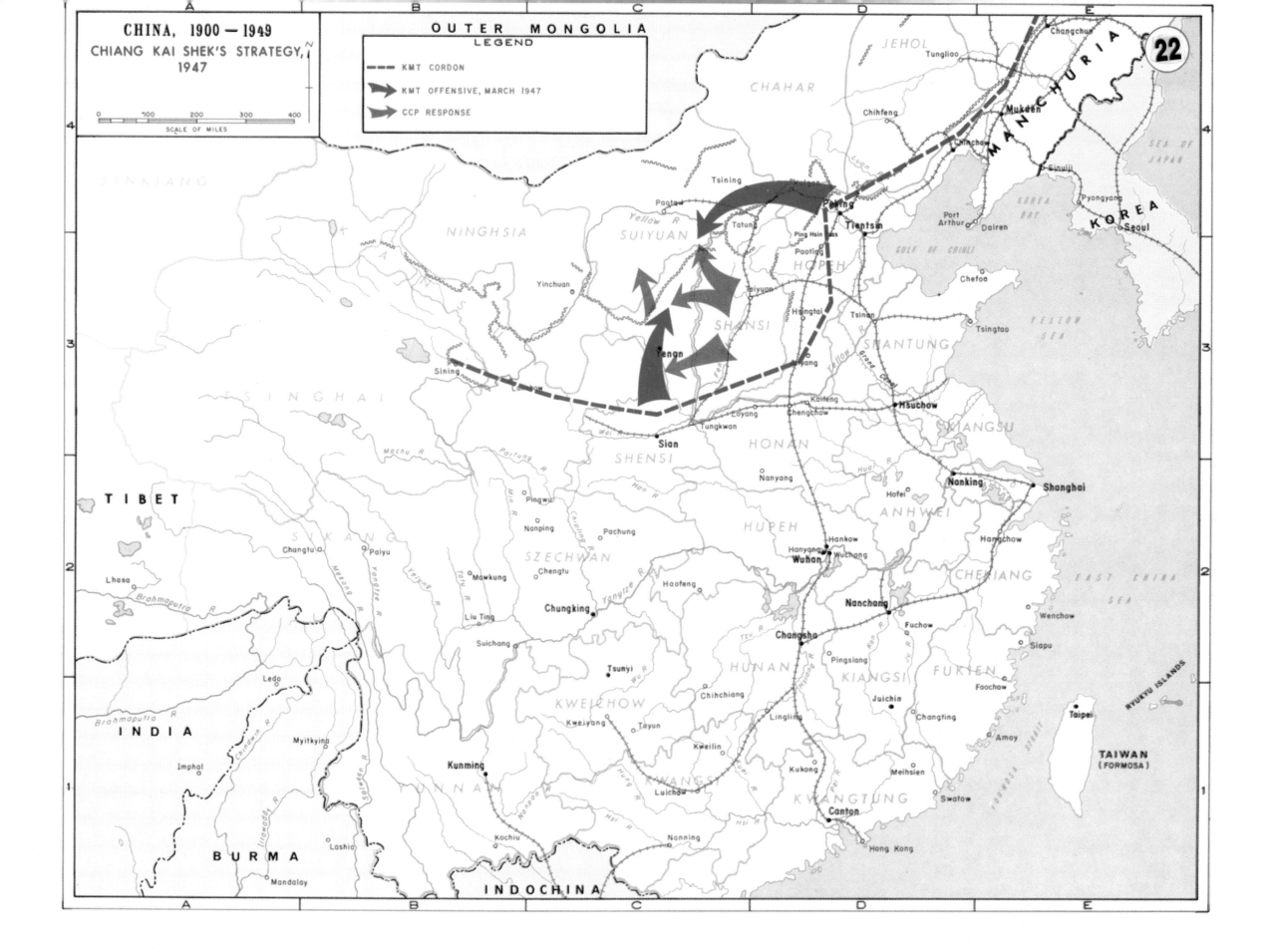

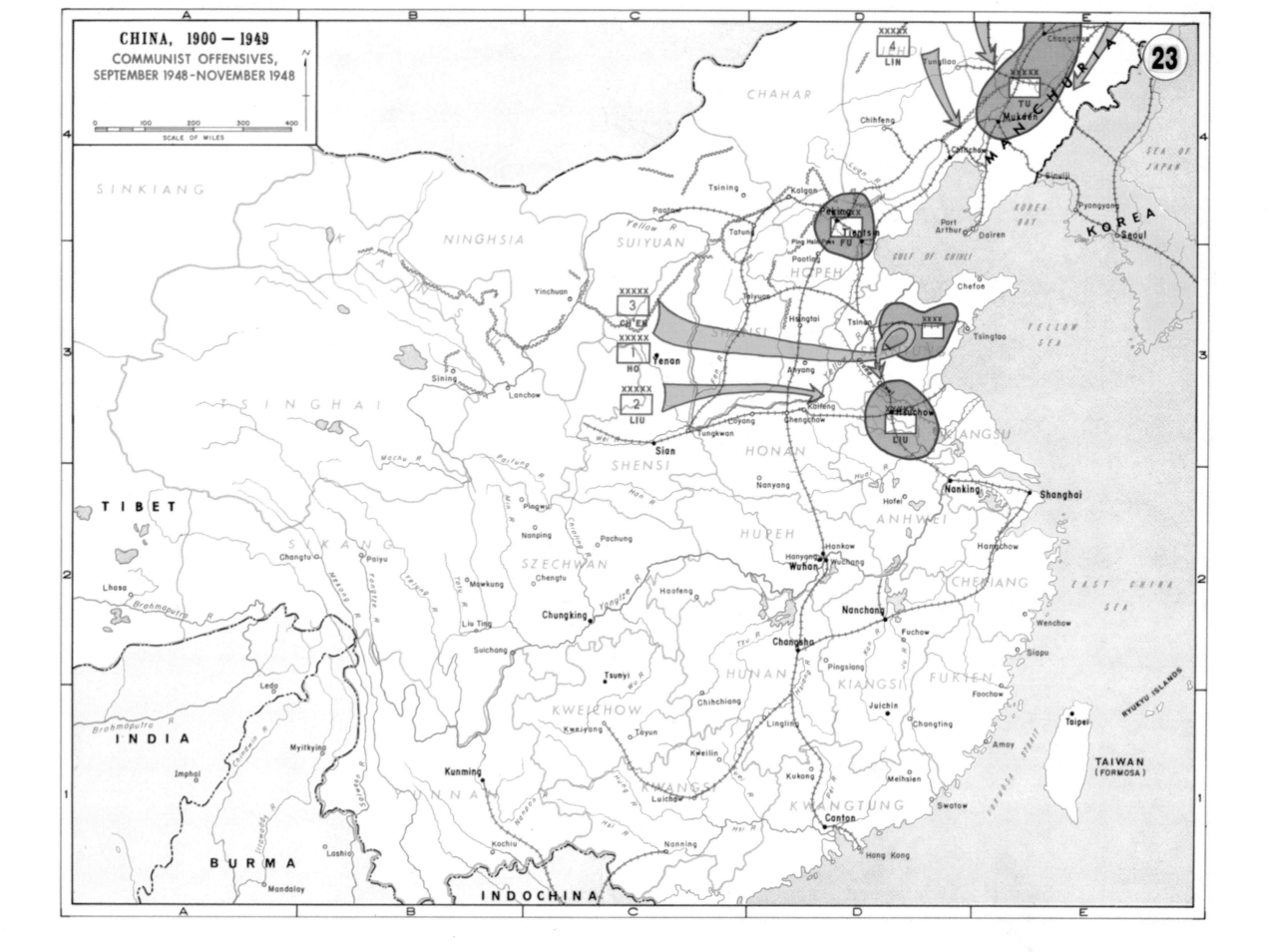

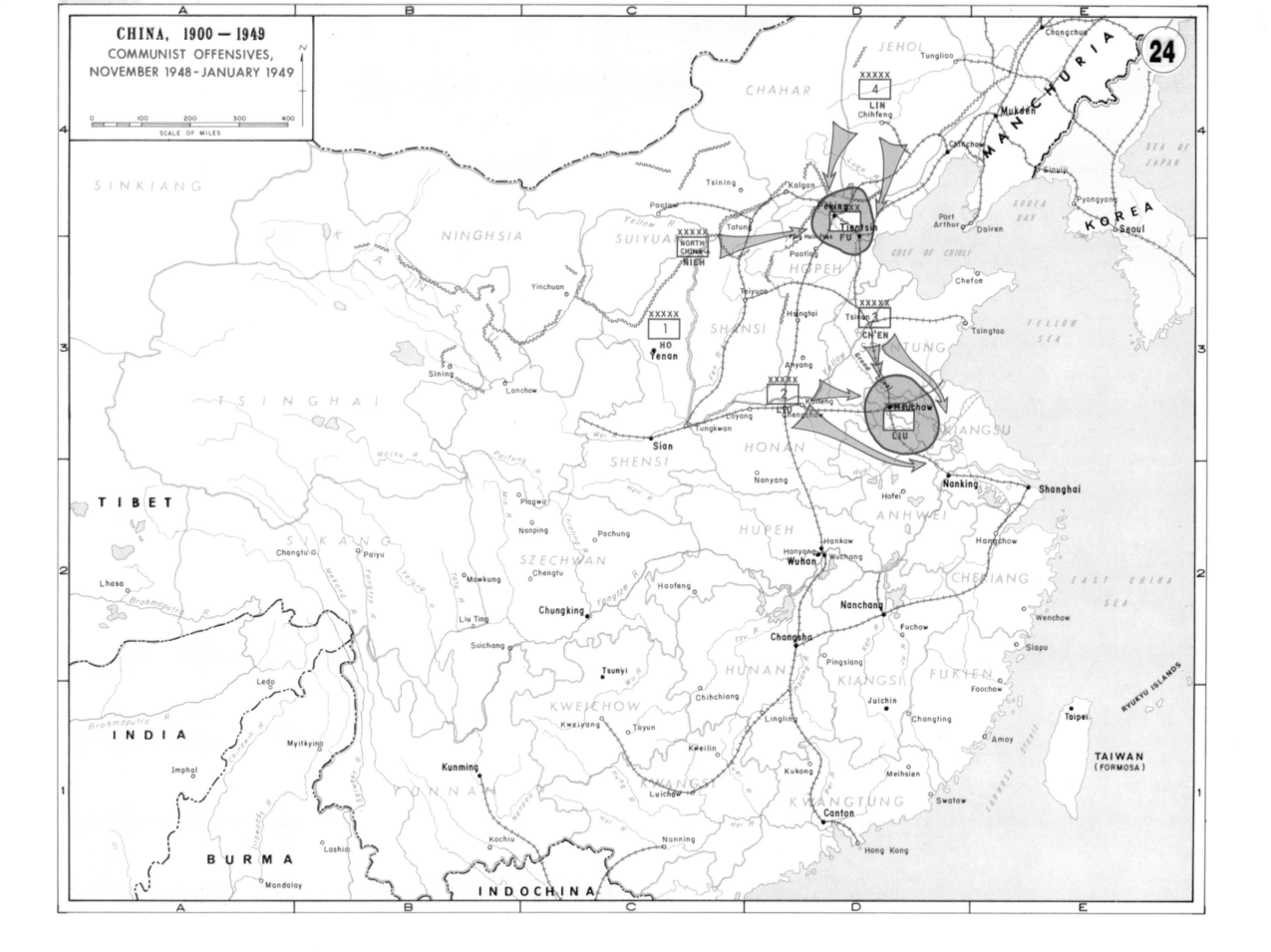

SCALE OF MILES

0   100   200   300   400

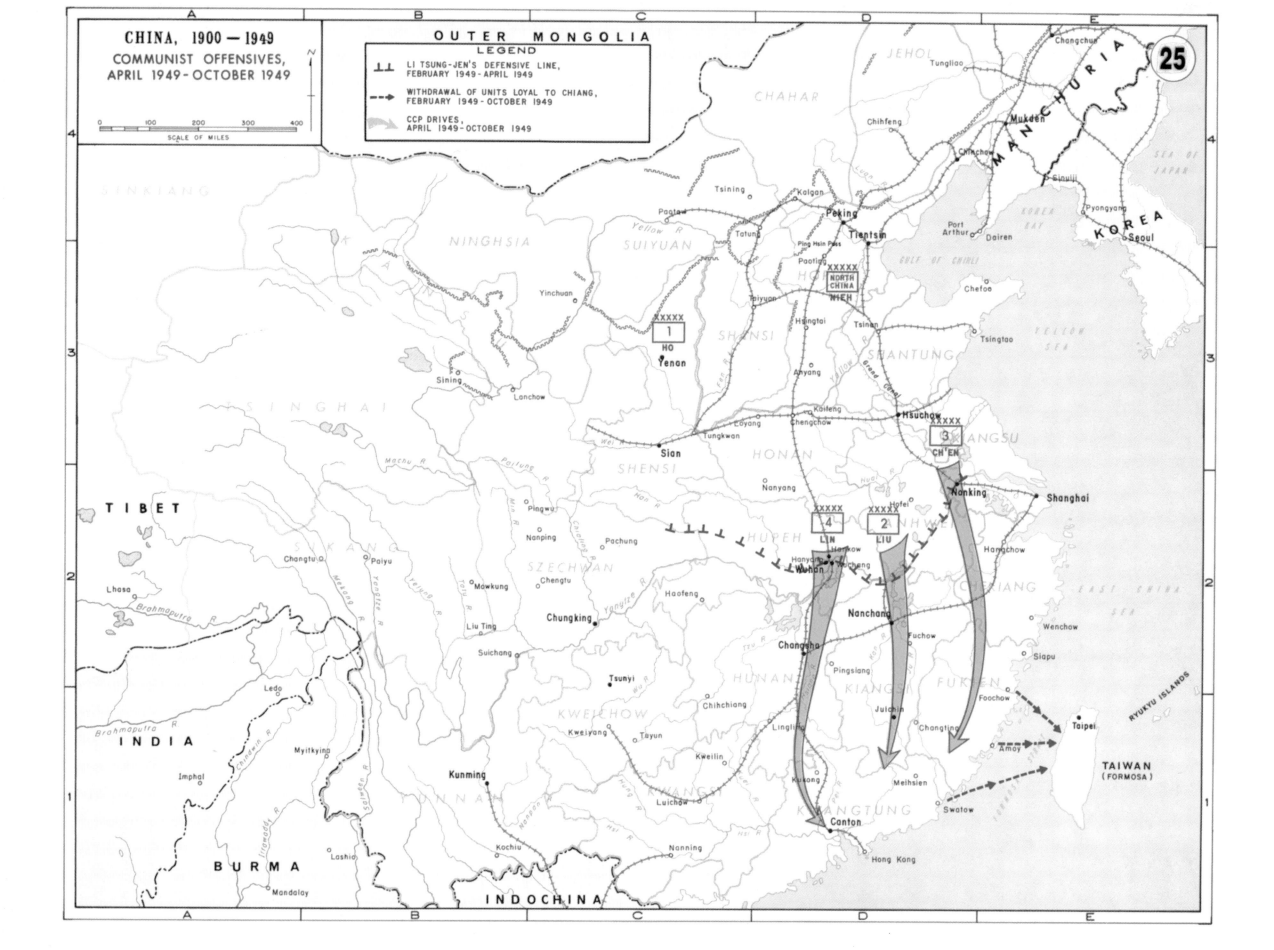

CHINA, 1900 — 1949
COMMUNIST OFFENSIVES,
APRIL 1949 - OCTOBER 1949

LEGEND

⊥⊥ LI TSUNG-JEN'S DEFENSIVE LINE,
FEBRUARY 1949 - APRIL 1949

- - → WITHDRAWAL OF UNITS LOYAL TO CHIANG,
FEBRUARY 1949 - OCTOBER 1949

CCP DRIVES,
APRIL 1949 - OCTOBER 1949

SCALE OF MILES
0   100   200   300   400

The Korean War

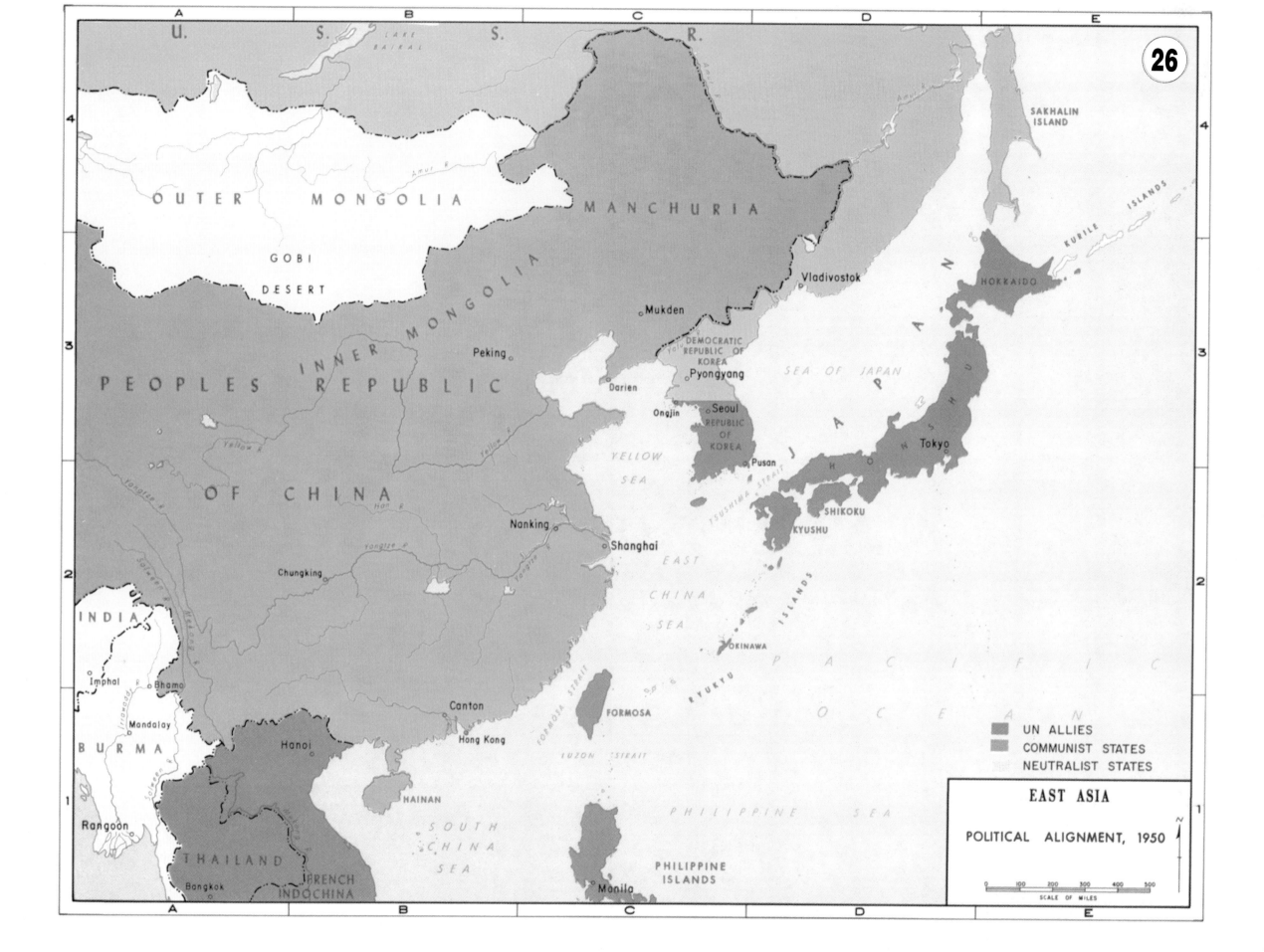

EAST ASIA

POLITICAL ALIGNMENT, 1950

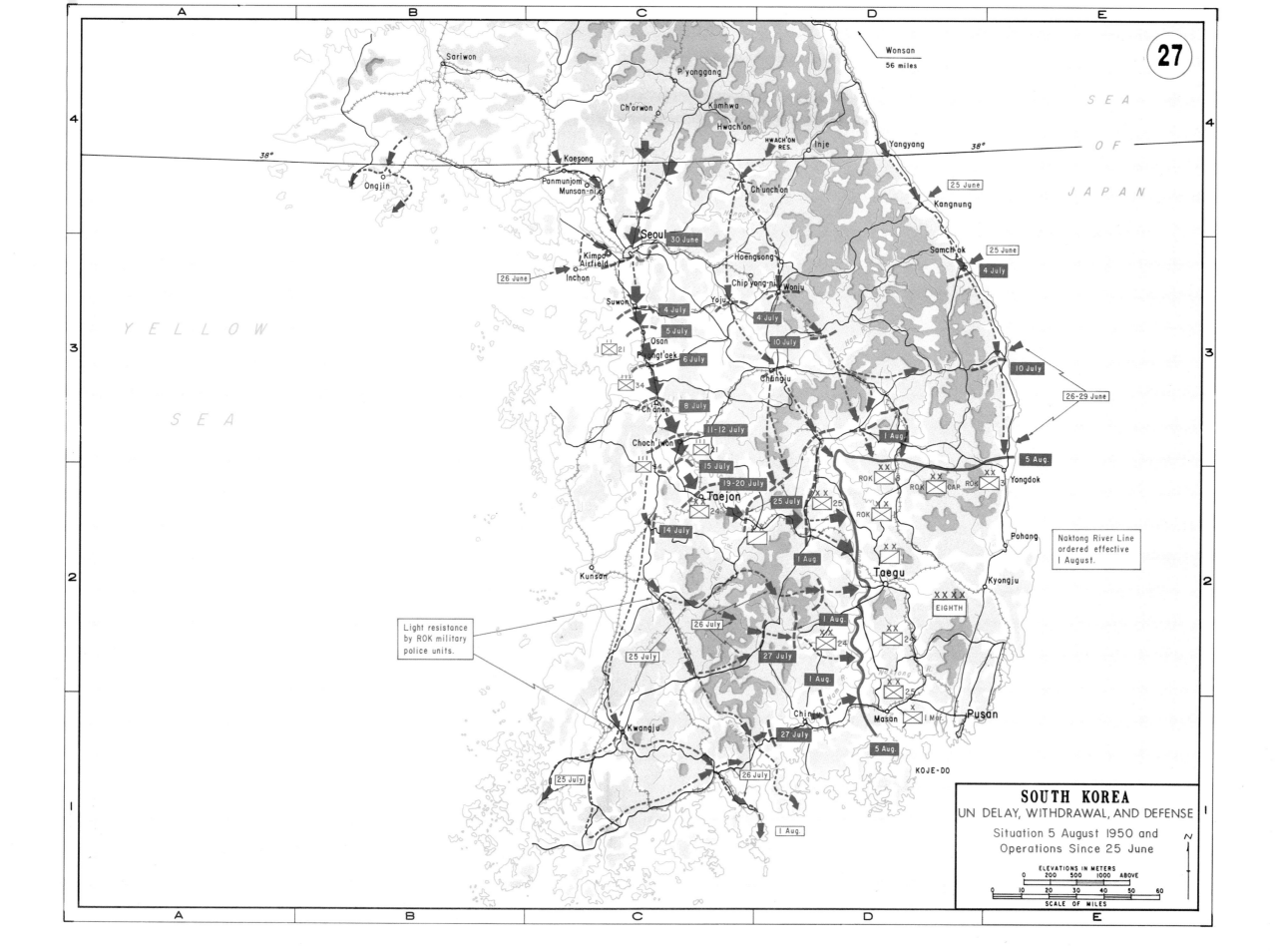

SOUTH KOREA
UN DELAY, WITHDRAWAL, AND DEFENSE
Situation 5 August 1950 and
Operations Since 25 June

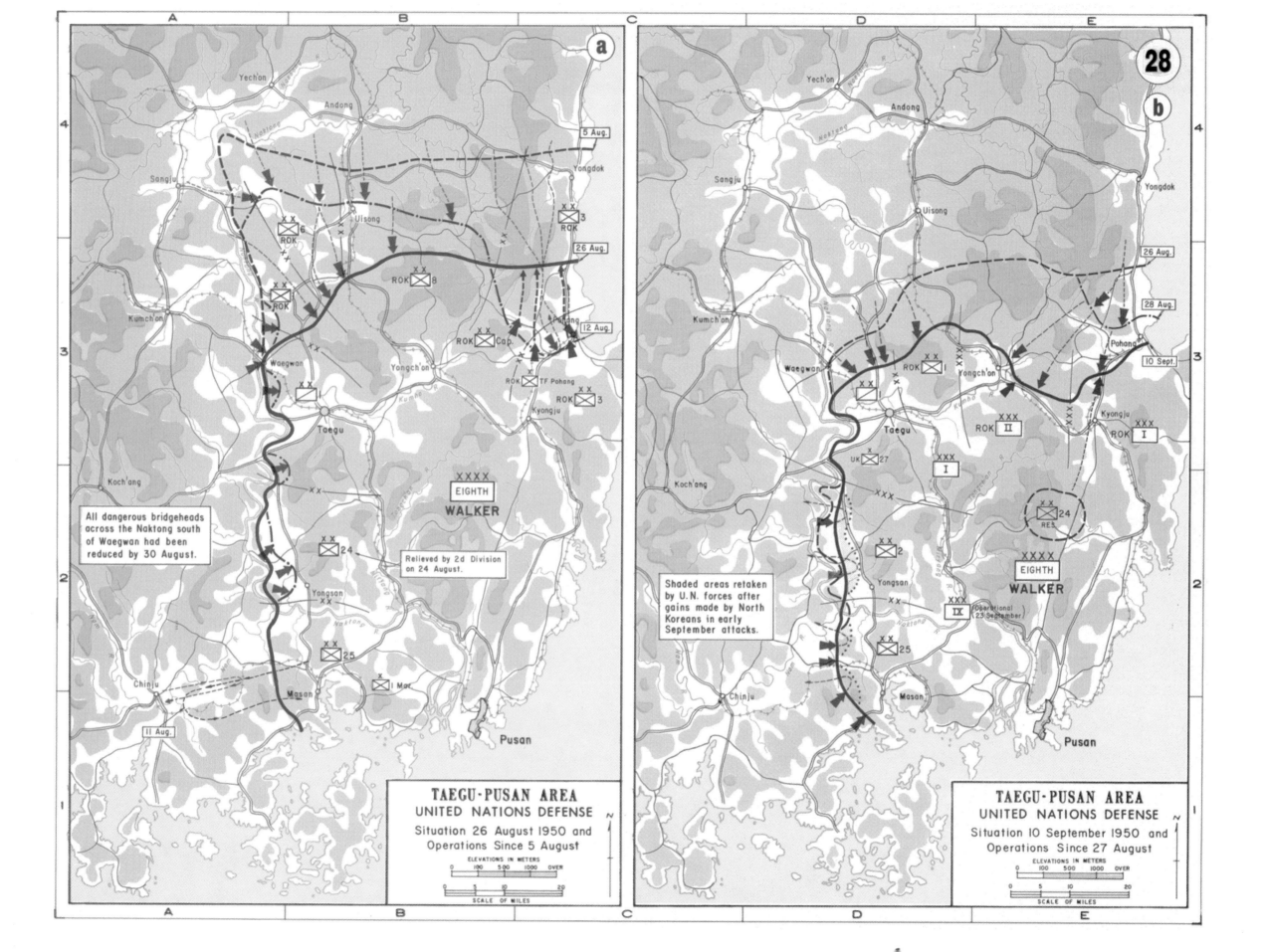

a

5 Aug.

Yech'on

Andong

Naktong R.

Sangju

Yongdok

XX 6 ROK

Uisong

XX 3 ROK

26 Aug.

XX ROK

ROK XX 8

XX

Kumch'on

ROK XX Cap.

Waegwan

12 Aug.

XX

Yongch'on

ROK TF Pohang

Kemar R.

ROK XX 3

Taegu

Kyongju

Koch'ang

XXXX
EIGHTH
WALKER

All dangerous bridgeheads across the Naktong south of Waegwan had been reduced by 30 August.

XX 24

Naktong R.

Yongsan
XX

Relieved by 2d Division on 24 August.

Naktong R.

Chinju

XX 25

Masan

X I Mar.

Pusan

11 Aug.

TAEGU-PUSAN AREA
UNITED NATIONS DEFENSE
Situation 26 August 1950 and
Operations Since 5 August

ELEVATIONS IN METERS
0 100 500 1000 OVER

0 5 10 20
SCALE OF MILES

b

28

Yech'on

Naktong R.

Andong

Sangju

Uisong

Yongdok

26 Aug.

28 Aug.

Kumch'on

Waegwan

XX ROK I

Yongch'on

Pohang

XX

10 Sept.

Taegu

ROK II XXX

Kyongju

ROK I XXX

UK X 27

XXX I

XX 24 RES

Koch'ang

XX 2

Yongsan

XXXX
EIGHTH
WALKER

Shaded areas retaken by U.N. forces after gains made by North Koreans in early September attacks.

Nam R.

Naktong R.

XXX IX
Operational 23 September

XX 25

Chinju

Masan

Pusan

TAEGU-PUSAN AREA
UNITED NATIONS DEFENSE
Situation 10 September 1950 and
Operations Since 27 August

ELEVATIONS IN METERS
0 100 500 1000 OVER

0 5 10 20
SCALE OF MILES

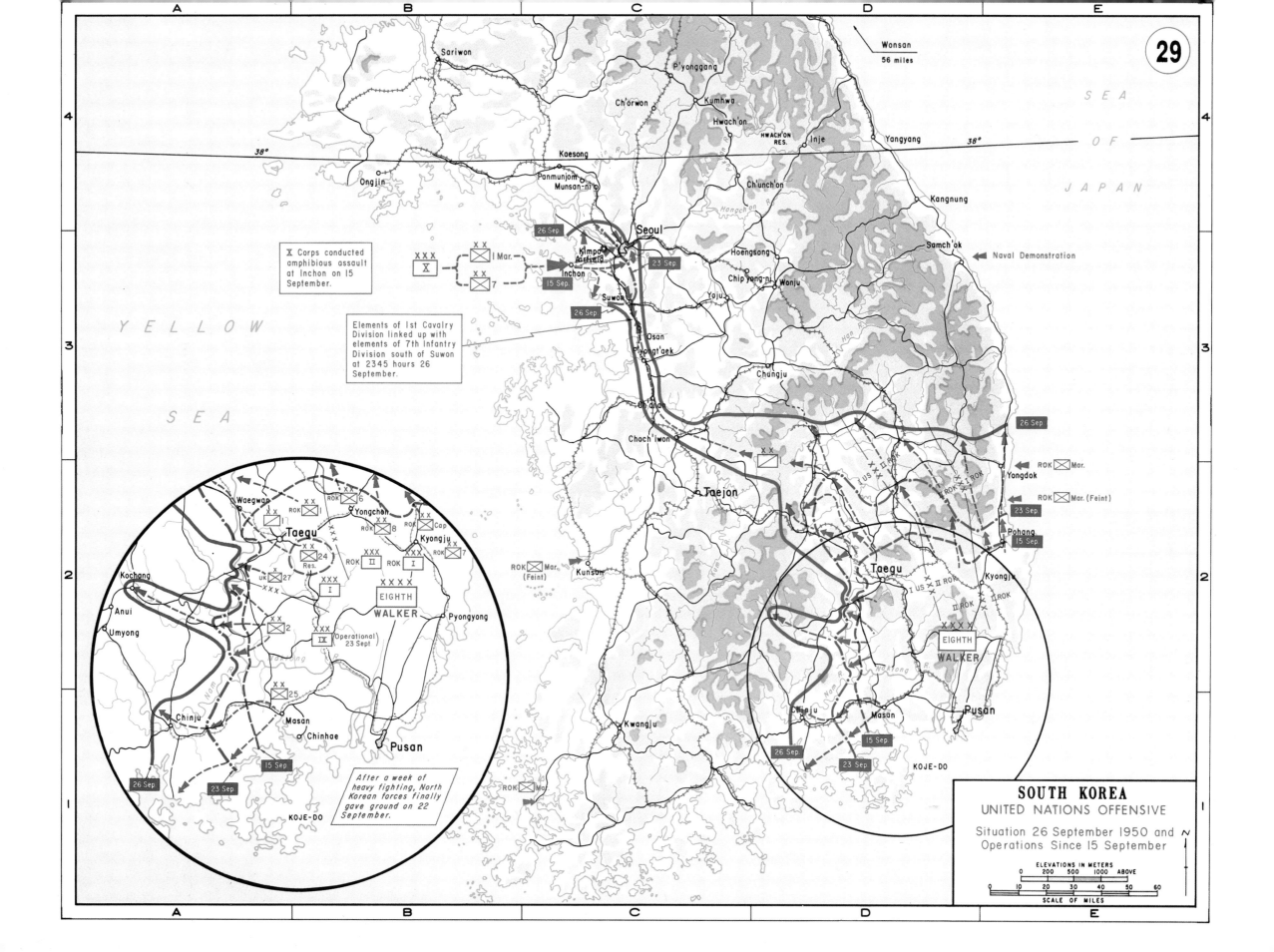

29

SOUTH KOREA
UNITED NATIONS OFFENSIVE
Situation 26 September 1950 and
Operations Since 15 September

X Corps conducted amphibious assault at Inchon on 15 September.

Elements of 1st Cavalry Division linked up with elements of 7th Infantry Division south of Suwon at 2345 hours 26 September.

After a week of heavy fighting, North Korean forces finally gave ground on 22 September.

ELEVATIONS IN METERS
0   200 500 1000 ABOVE

SCALE OF MILES

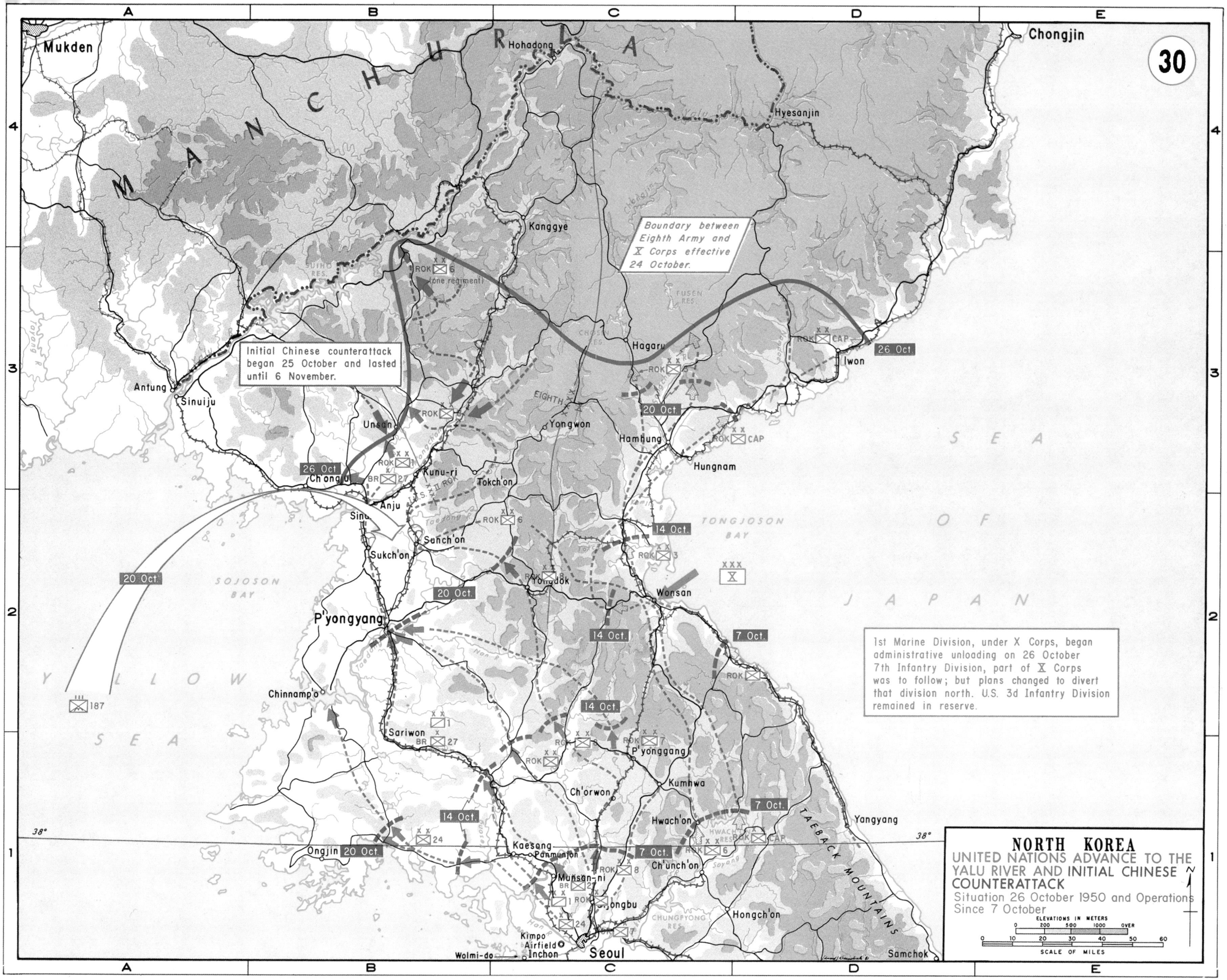
30
NORTH KOREA
UNITED NATIONS ADVANCE TO THE YALU RIVER AND INITIAL CHINESE COUNTERATTACK
Situation 26 October 1950 and Operations Since 7 October
ELEVATIONS IN METERS
0 200 500 1000 OVER
SCALE OF MILES
0 10 20 30 40 50 60
Boundary between Eighth Army and X Corps effective 24 October.
Initial Chinese counterattack began 25 October and lasted until 6 November.
1st Marine Division, under X Corps, began administrative unloading on 26 October 7th Infantry Division, part of X Corps was to follow; but plans changed to divert that division north. U.S. 3d Infantry Division remained in reserve.
MANCHURIA
Mukden
Hohadong
Chongjin
Hyesanjin
Kanggye
Hagaru
Iwon
Antung
Sinuiju
Unsan
Yongwon
Hamhung
Hungnam
Ch'ongju
Kunu-ri
Tokch'on
Anju
Sunch'on
Sukch'on
Yongdok
Wonsan
P'yongyang
Chinnamp'o
Sariwon
P'yonggang
Kumhwa
Ch'orwon
Hwach'on
Yangyang
Kaesang
Panmunjon
Ch'unch'on
Munsan-ni
Uijongbu
Hongch'on
Ongjin
Kimpo Airfield
Inchon
Wolmi-do
Seoul
Samchok
SEA OF JAPAN
YELLOW SEA
TONGJOSON BAY
SOJOSON BAY
TAEBACK MOUNTAINS
26 Oct.
20 Oct.
14 Oct.
7 Oct.
ROK
CAP
BR 27
187
24
38°
A B C D E
1 2 3 4

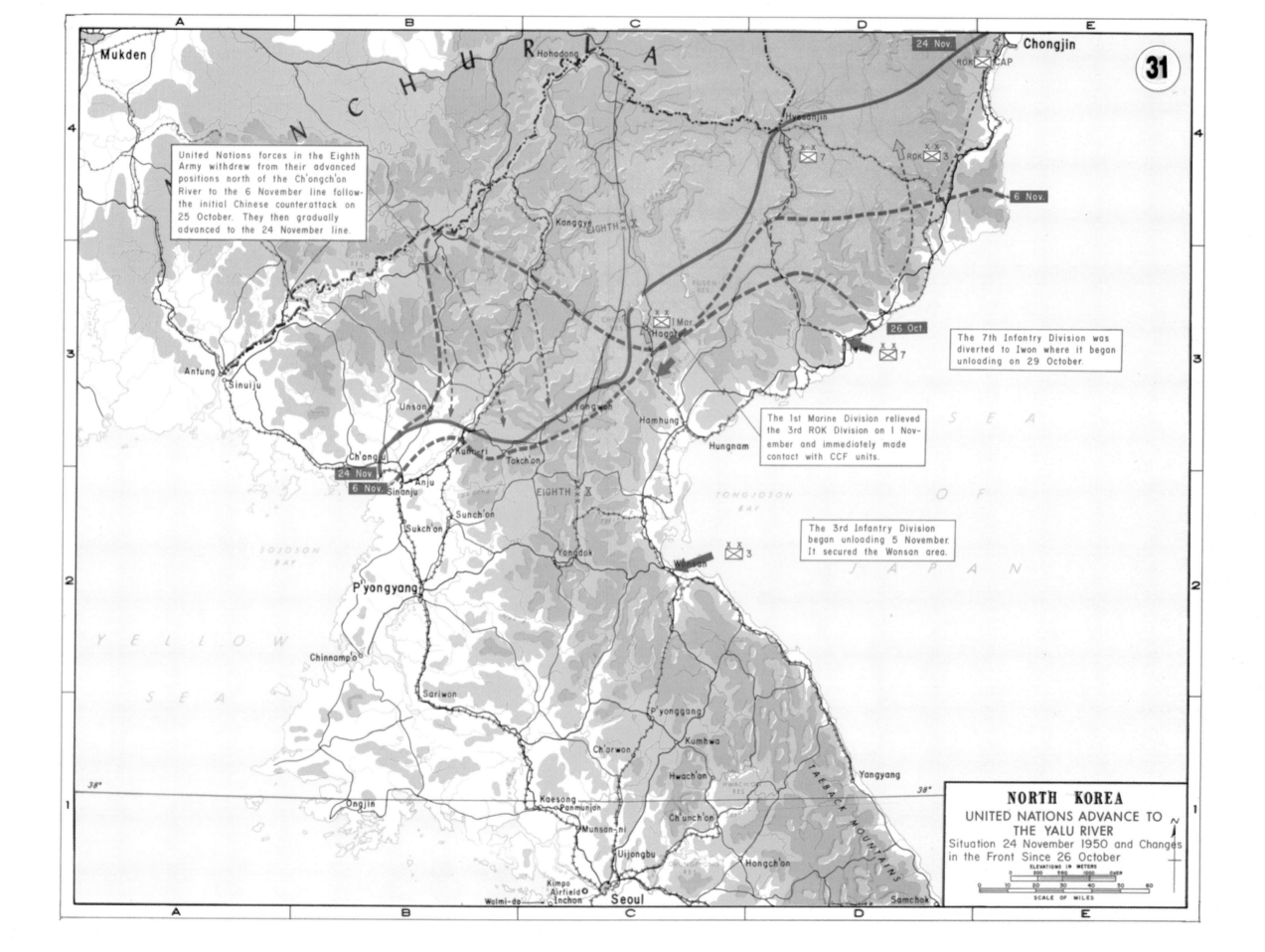

United Nations forces in the Eighth
Army withdrew from their advanced
positions north of the Ch'ongch'on
River to the 6 November line follow-
the initial Chinese counterattack on
25 October. They then gradually
advanced to the 24 November line.

The 7th Infantry Division was
diverted to Iwon where it began
unloading on 29 October.

The 1st Marine Division relieved
the 3rd ROK Division on 1 November and immediately made
contact with CCF units.

The 3rd Infantry Division
began unloading 5 November.
It secured the Wonsan area.

24 Nov.

6 Nov.

26 Oct.

NORTH KOREA

UNITED NATIONS ADVANCE TO
THE YALU RIVER

Situation 24 November 1950 and Changes
in the Front Since 26 October

ELEVATIONS IN METERS
200   500   1000   OVER

0   10   20   30   40   50   60

SCALE OF MILES

31

Mukden

MANCHURIA

Hohadong

Chongjin

ROK   CAP

Hyesanjin

XX   7

ROK   XX   3

Kanggye

EIGHTH   X

XX   1 Mar.
Hagaru

XX   7
Iwon

Antung

Sinuiju

Unsan

Yongwon

Hamhung

Hungnam

Ch'ongju

Kunu-ri   Tokch'on

SEA

24 Nov.
6 Nov.
Anju
Sinanju

EIGHTH   XX

TONGJOSON
BAY

OF

Sukch'on

Sunch'on

XX   3
Wonsan

Yongdok

JAPAN

SOJOSON
BAY

P'yongyang

YELLOW

Chinnamp'o

SEA

Sariwon

P'yonggang

Kumhwa

Ch'orwon

Hwach'on

HWACH'ON
RES.

TAEBAECK   MOUNTAINS

Yangyang

38°

38°

Kaesong

Panmunjon

Ch'unch'on

Munsan-ni

Uijongbu

Hongch'on

Kimpo
Airfield

Wolmi-do   Inchon

Seoul

Samchok

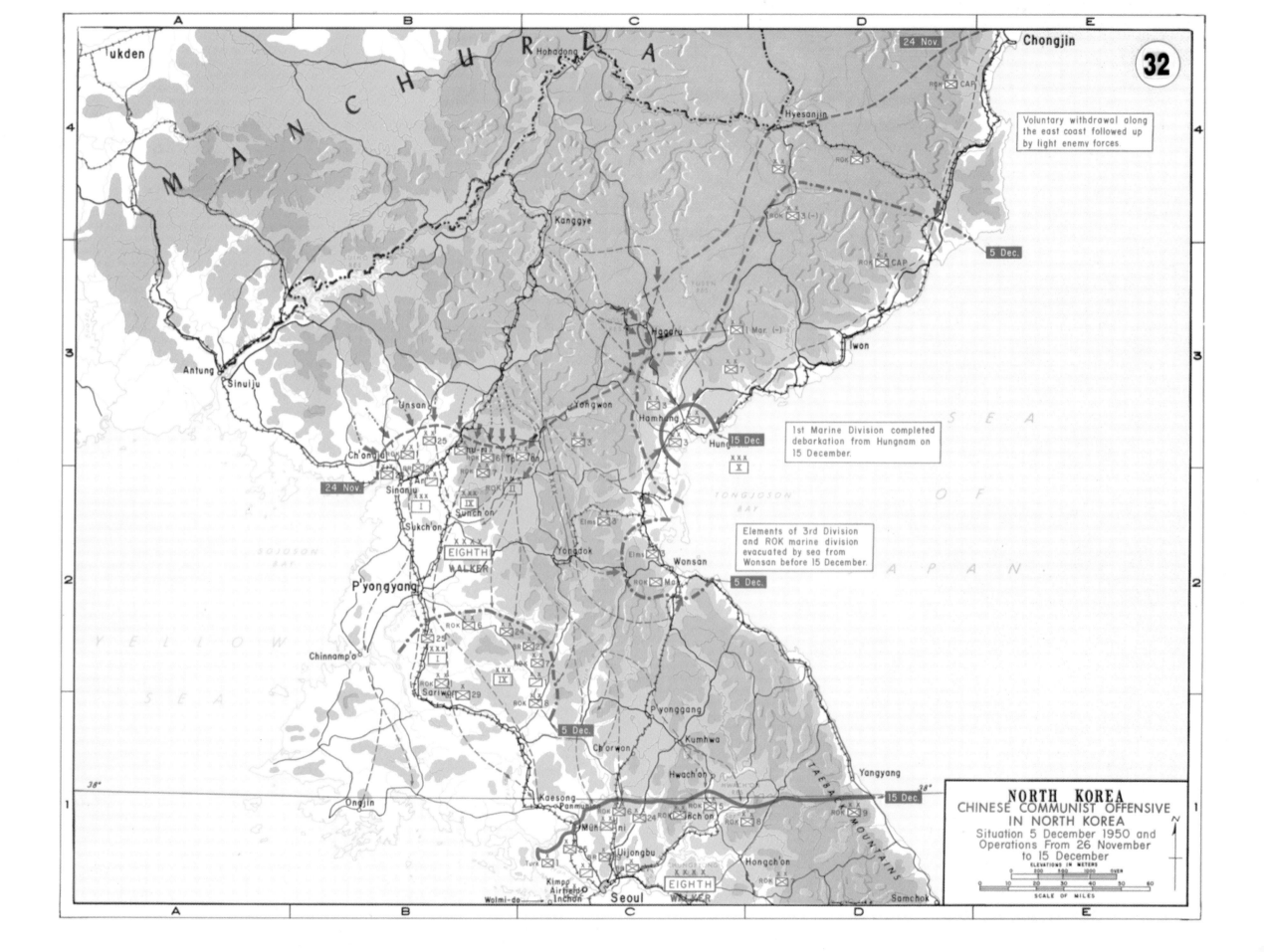

NORTH KOREA
CHINESE COMMUNIST OFFENSIVE
IN NORTH KOREA
Situation 5 December 1950 and
Operations From 26 November
to 15 December

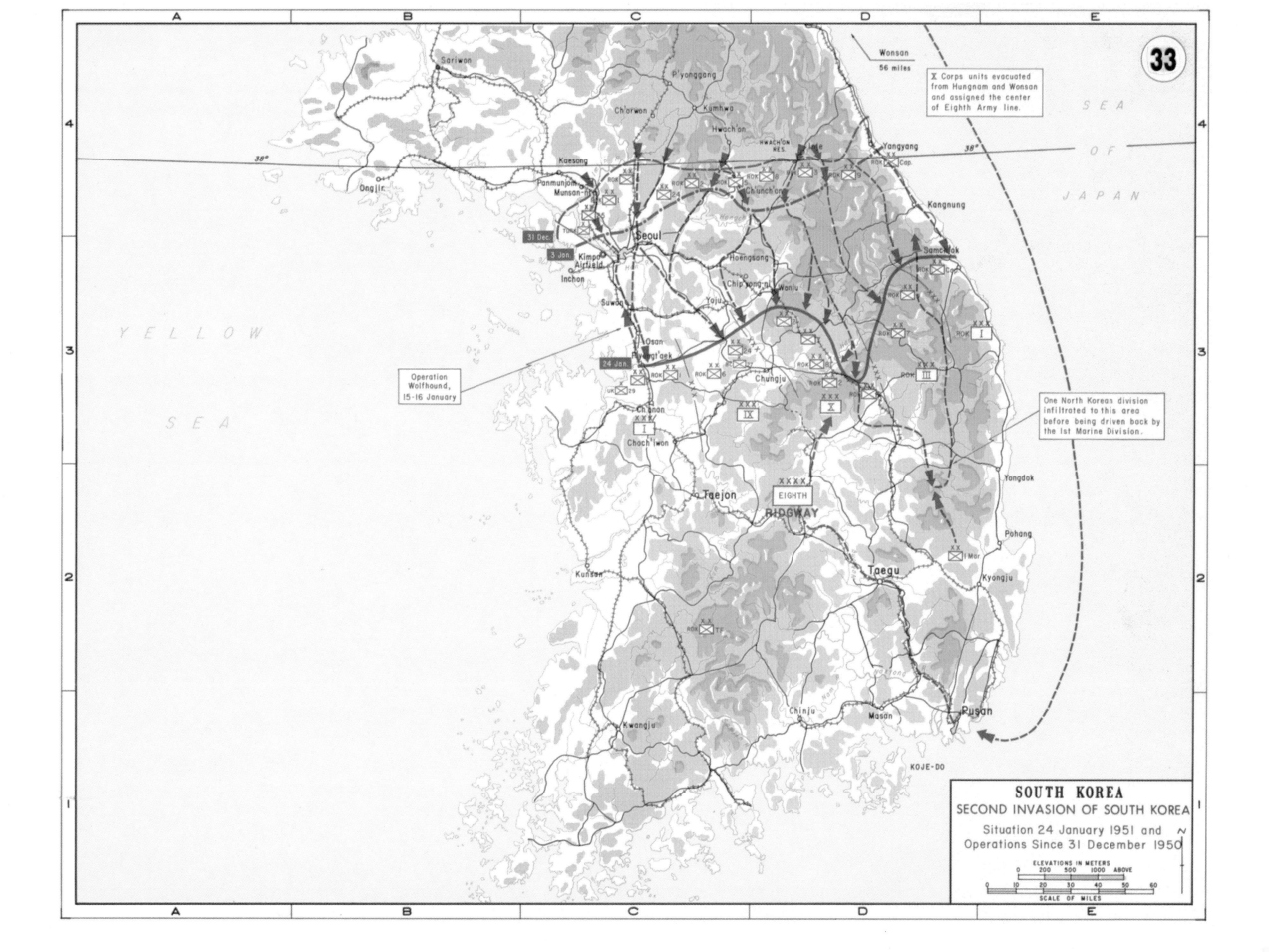

33

Wonsan
56 miles

X Corps units evacuated
from Hungnam and Wonsan
and assigned the center
of Eighth Army line.

One North Korean division
infiltrated to this area
before being driven back by
the 1st Marine Division.

Operation
Wolfhound,
15-16 January

31 Dec.

3 Jan.

24 Jan.

38°

38°

SEA OF JAPAN

YELLOW SEA

Sariwon
P'yonggang
Ch'orwon
Kumhwa
Hwach'on
HWACH'ON RES.
Kaesong
Panmunjom
Munsan-ni
Ch'unch'on
Yangyang
Kangnung
Seoul
Kimpo Airfield
Inchon
Hoengsong
Chip'yong-ni
Wonju
Samch'ok
Suwon
Yoju
Osan
P'yongt'aek
Chungju
Ch'onan
Choch'iwon
Taejon
EIGHTH
RIDGWAY
Kunsan
Taegu
Yongdok
Pohang
Kyongju
Kwangju
Chinju
Masan
Pusan
KOJE-DO

IX
X
I
III
I

SOUTH KOREA
SECOND INVASION OF SOUTH KOREA

Situation 24 January 1951 and
Operations Since 31 December 1950

ELEVATIONS IN METERS
0   200   500   1000   ABOVE

0   10   20   30   40   50   60
SCALE OF MILES

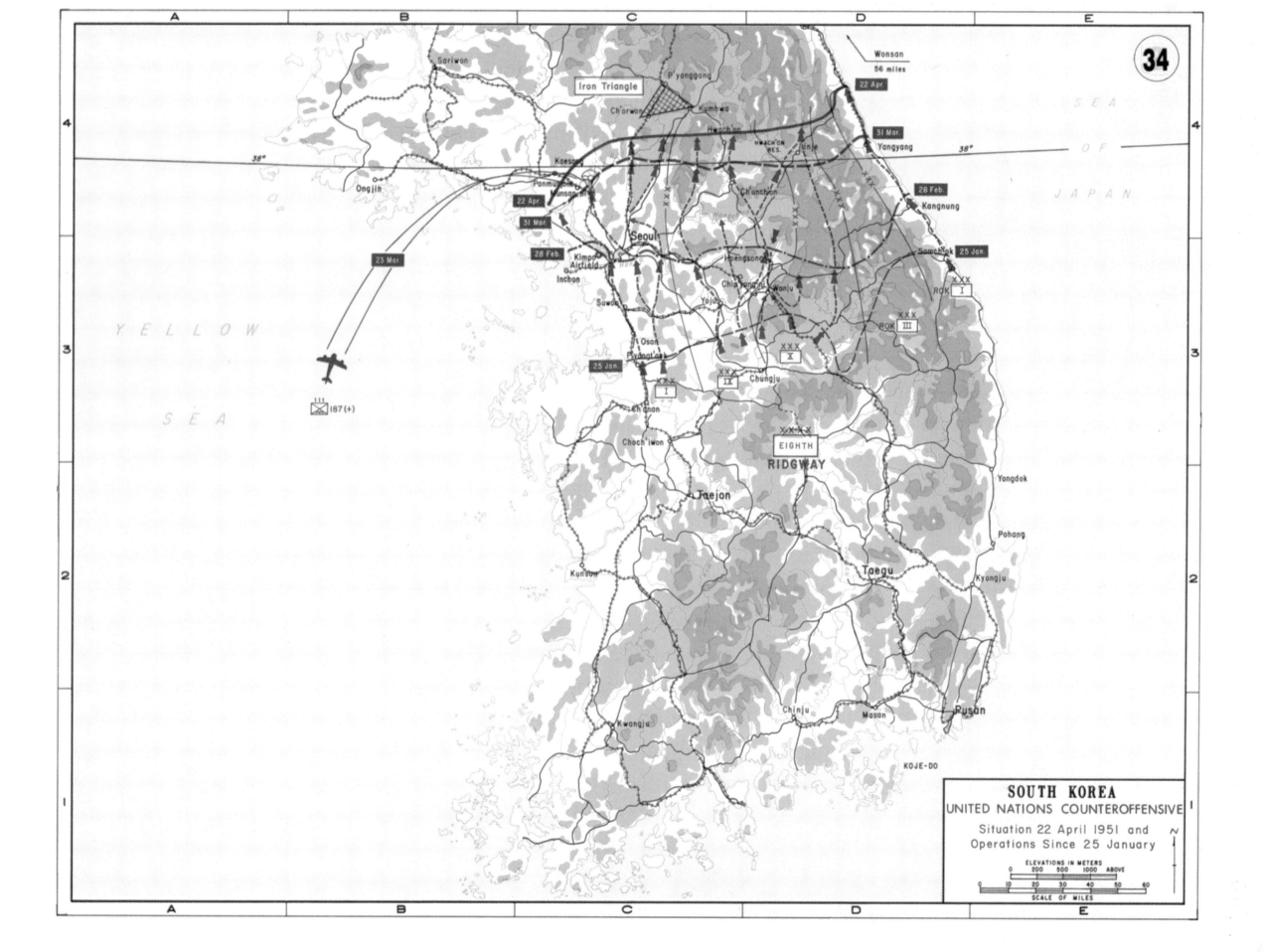

SOUTH KOREA
UNITED NATIONS COUNTEROFFENSIVE
Situation 22 April 1951 and
Operations Since 25 January

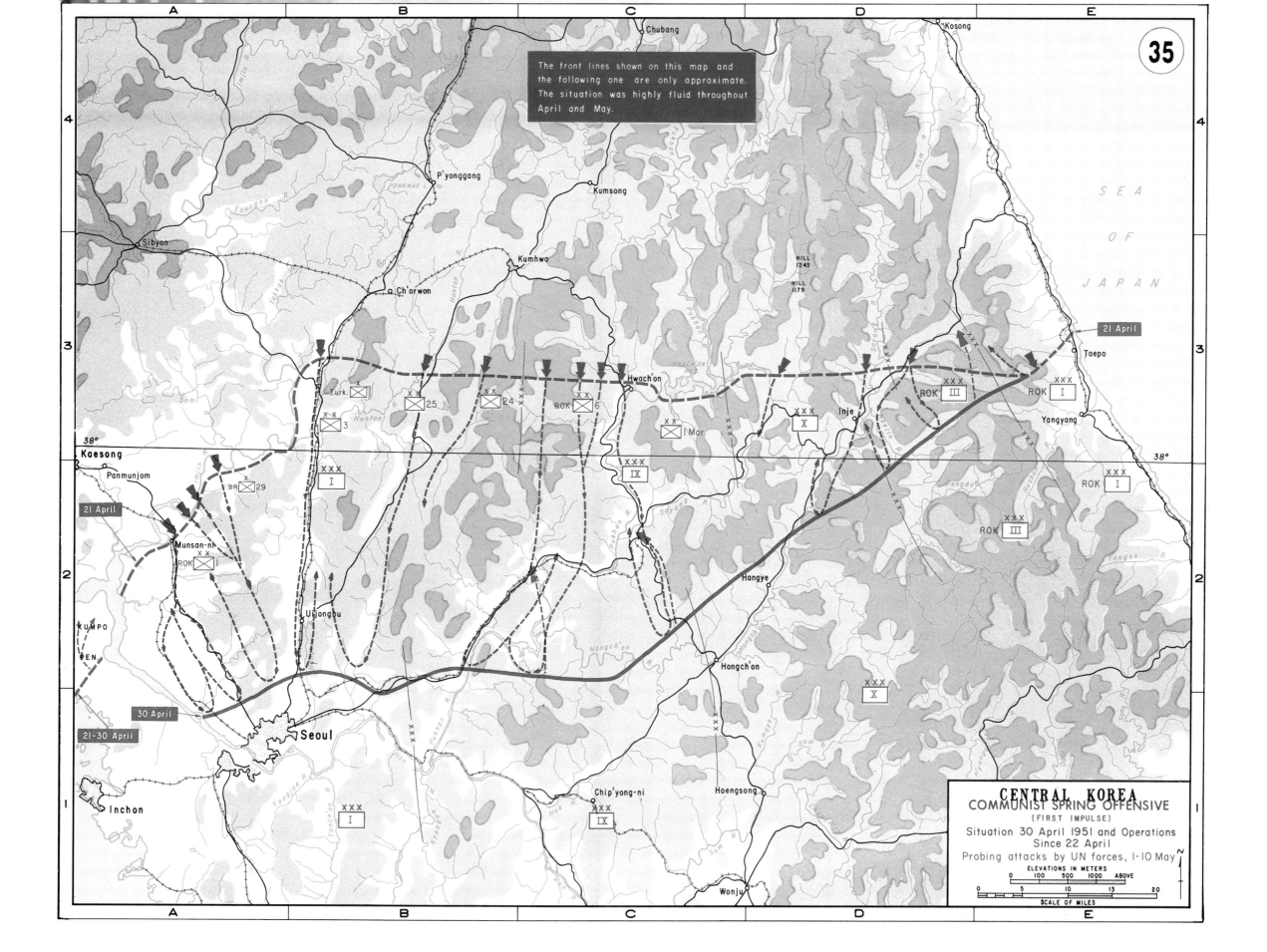

The front lines shown on this map and the following one are only approximate. The situation was highly fluid throughout April and May.

SEA

OF

JAPAN

Chubang

Kosong

35

21 April

Taepo

P'yonggang

Kumsong

HILL
1243

HILL
1179

Sibyon

Kumhwa

XXX

ROK ⫿ III

ROK ⫿ I

Ch'orwon

Hwach'on

XX
Turk. ⊠

XX 25
⊠

XX 24
⊠ XXX

ROK ⊠ 6

XXX

ROK ⫿ III

Yangyang

Inje

38°

X

38°

Kaesong

XX
⊠ 3

XX
1 Mar.

XXX

XXX

X

Panmunjom

I

XXX

IX

XXX

ROK ⫿ I

BR ⊠ 29

21 April

Munsan-ni

ROK ⊠ I

Hangye

Uijongbu

KUMPO
PEN.

Hongch'on

30 April

Hongch'on

XXX
X

21-30 April

Seoul

Chip'yong-ni

Hoengsong

Inchon

XXX
I

XXX
IX

CENTRAL KOREA
COMMUNIST SPRING OFFENSIVE
(FIRST IMPULSE)
Situation 30 April 1951 and Operations
Since 22 April
Probing attacks by UN forces, 1-10 May

Wonju

ELEVATIONS IN METERS
100   500   1000   ABOVE

0   5   10   15   20
SCALE OF MILES

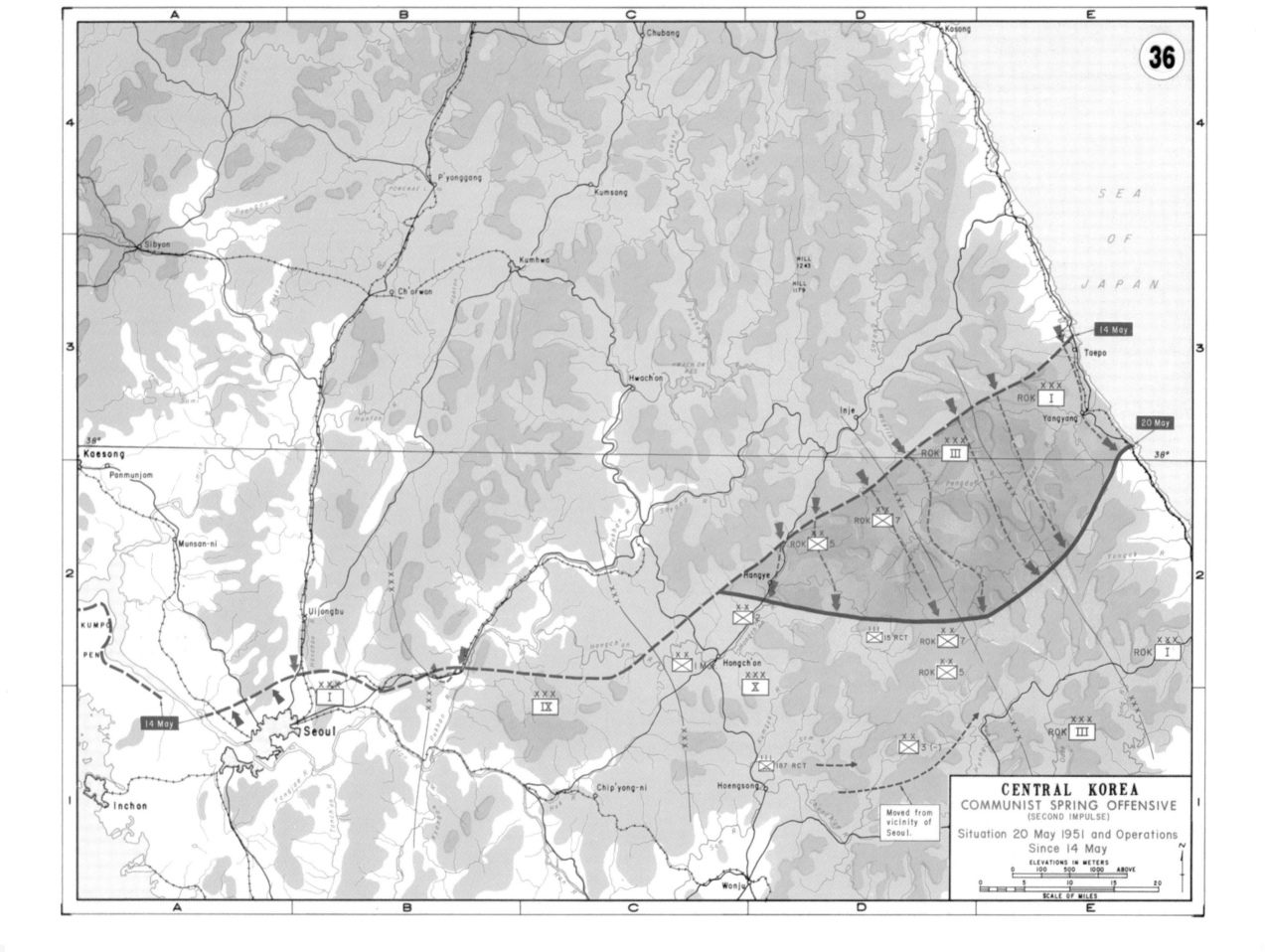

CENTRAL KOREA
COMMUNIST SPRING OFFENSIVE
(SECOND IMPULSE)

Situation 20 May 1951 and Operations
Since 14 May

ELEVATIONS IN METERS

0   100   500   1000   ABOVE

0   5   10   15   20
SCALE OF MILES

36

Moved from
vicinity of
Seoul.

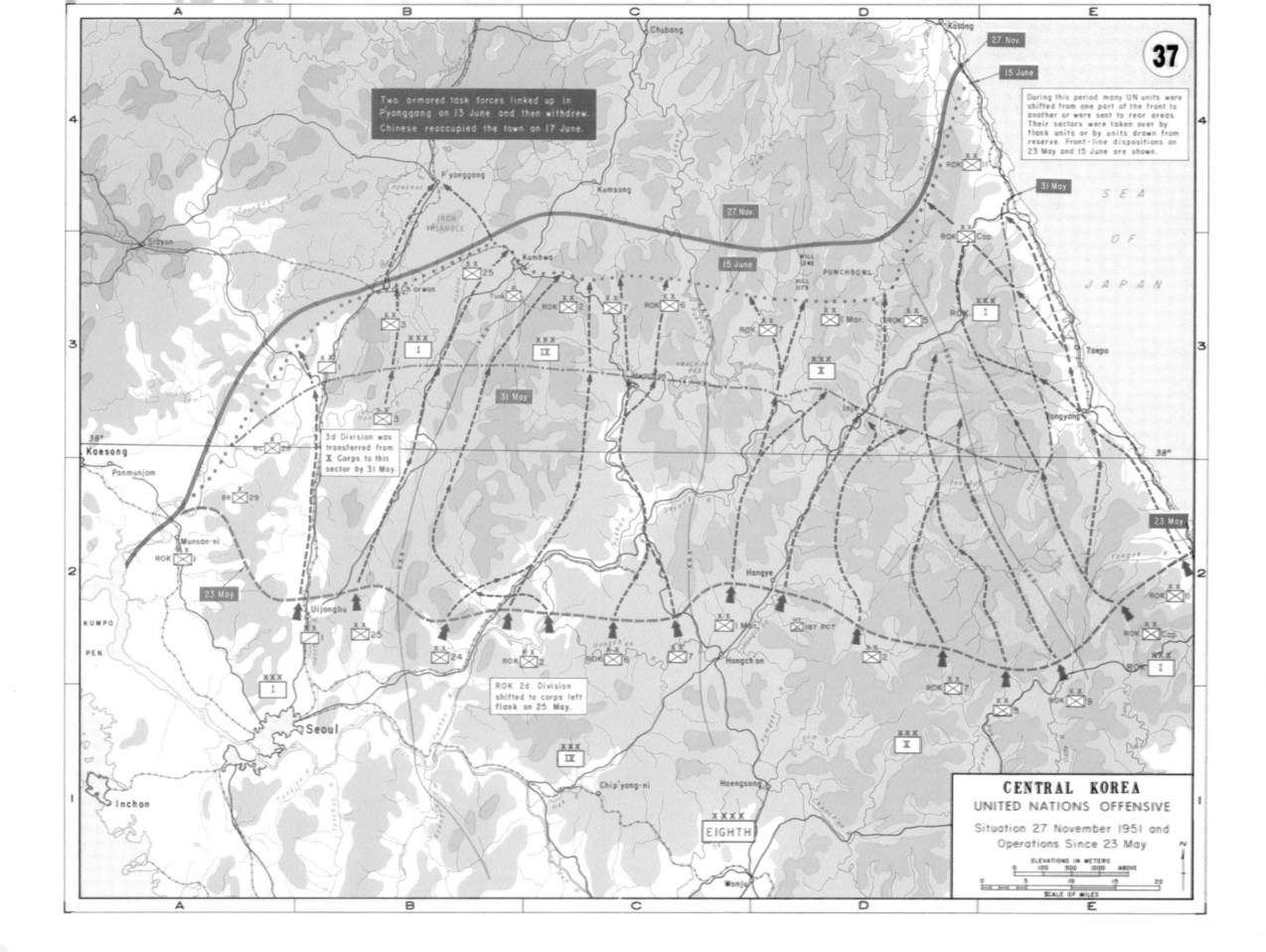

37

Two armored task forces linked up in Pyonggang on 13 June and then withdrew. Chinese reoccupied the town on 17 June.

During this period many UN units were shifted from one part of the front to another or were sent to rear areas. Their sectors were taken over by flank units or by units drawn from reserve. Front-line dispositions on 23 May and 15 June are shown.

27 Nov.

15 June

31 May

23 May

3d Division was transferred from X Corps to this sector by 31 May.

ROK 2d Division shifted to corps left flank on 25 May.

SEA OF JAPAN

IRON TRIANGLE

PUNCHBOWL

CENTRAL KOREA
UNITED NATIONS OFFENSIVE

Situation 27 November 1951 and
Operations Since 23 May

ELEVATIONS IN METERS
100   500   1000   ABOVE

SCALE OF MILES
0   5   10   15   20

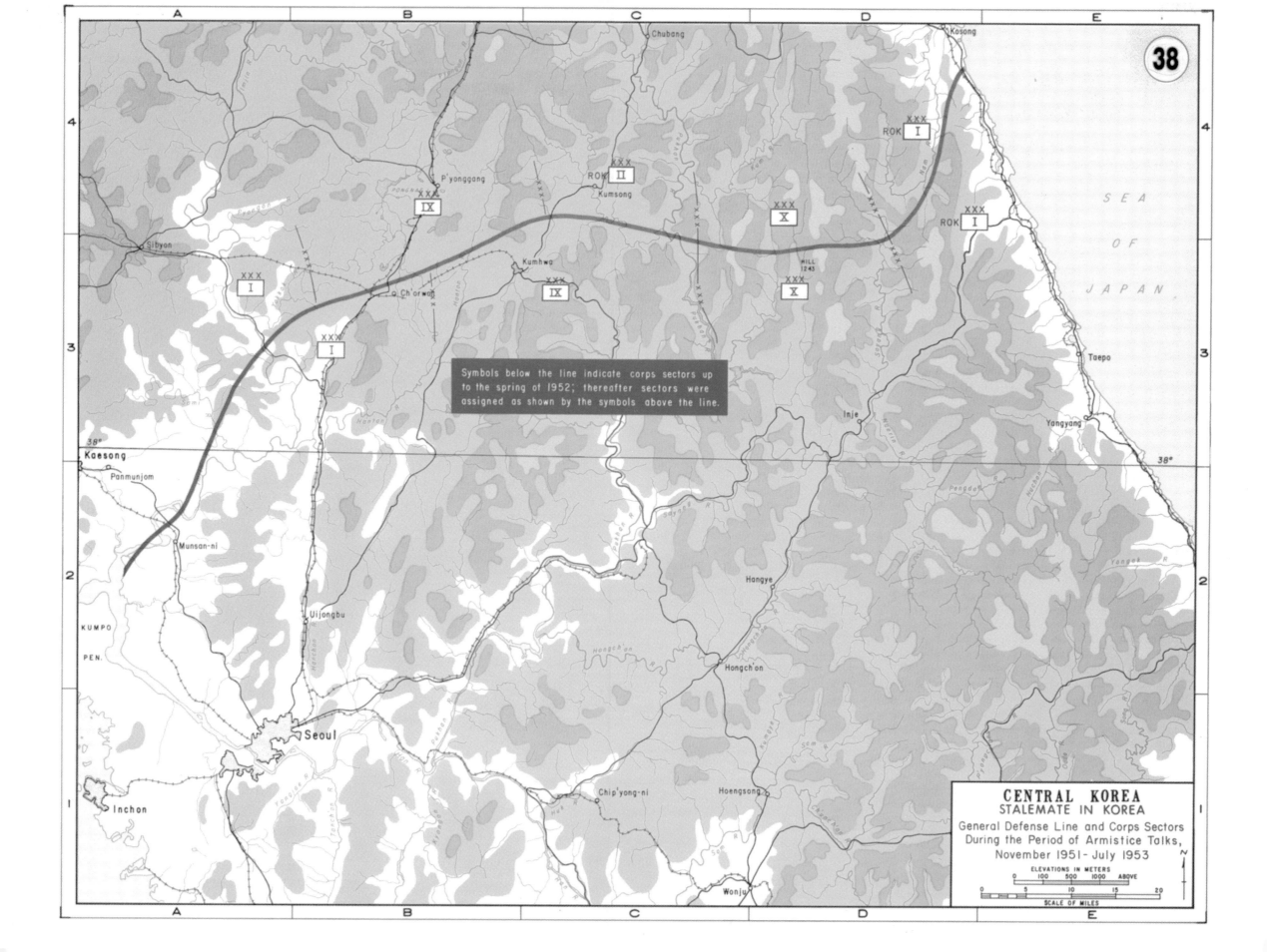

38

Symbols below the line indicate corps sectors up to the spring of 1952; thereafter sectors were assigned as shown by the symbols above the line.

SEA

OF

JAPAN

Chubang

Kosong

ROK XXX I

P'yonggang

ROK XXX II

Kumsong

XXX IX

ROK XXX I

Sibyon

XXX X

XXX I

Kumhwa

Taepo

Ch'orwan

XXX IX

HILL 1243

XXX X

38°

Kaesong

38°

Inje

Panmunjom

Yangyang

KUMPO PEN.

Munsan-ni

Hangye

Uijongbu

Hongch'on

KUMPO PEN.

Seoul

Inchon

Chip'yong-ni

Hoengsong

CENTRAL KOREA
STALEMATE IN KOREA

General Defense Line and Corps Sectors
During the Period of Armistice Talks,
November 1951 - July 1953

Wonju

ELEVATIONS IN METERS
0   100   500   1000   ABOVE

0   5   10   15   20
SCALE OF MILES